Tales of a Free Spirit

by

Gavin Dobson

Librario

TALES OF A FREE SPIRIT

Published by

Librario Publishing Ltd

ISBN: 1-904440-66-5

Copies can be ordered via the Internet
www.librario.com

or from:

Brough House, Milton Brodie, Kinloss
Moray IV36 2UA
Tel /Fax No 00 44 (0)1343 850 617

for

Terrill, Henry, Olivia and Sa

…now you know what I was doing in my cave all that time

Table of Contents

Amo

to a little Egyptian girl long ago

Geordie's older brother was in a sanatorium in the Swiss Alps recovering from a bout of pneumonia. His father was gadding about Paris with the fast set, preoccupied with his horse at Longchamps and his mistress in St Cloud. His mother was distraught and could only stave off a nervous breakdown by working brutal hours as a translator around the world from Montevideo to Geneva. Anything, anywhere, to distract from the shattering truth that her marriage had collapsed into dust.

It was left to Geordie's Edinburgh grandmother to extract the bemused little boy from the wreckage. She collected him early one February morning in St Germain a week after his sixth birthday. He wore a camel hair duffel coat, pockets stuffed with the few toys he was allowed to take. His precious teddy bear was in one hand; the other was held tightly by his grandmother. The streets were dark when they left the house and the taxi raced across Paris on empty cobbles to the Gare du Nord.

By the time the train steamed into Calais it had developed into another grey murky maritime weekday. Sleety wind gusted from the north-west along the Channel and heavy smoke blew wildly from the ferry's funnels across the deck into the faces of the passengers. Scores of West Indians were crossing to England for the first time and many were retching over the railings even before the ship had slipped her moorings in Calais. They looked sad and out of place to the young boy, huddled in groups with their bright tropical clothes flapping crazily in the wintry gale. His grandmother found a warm place in a smoky lounge between decks and Geordie shared his toys with a petite

9

Jamaican girl, dressed only in a white shirt with short sleeves, a light skirt and cotton jacket. She had only ever known summer.

The ferry docked in Dover and the passengers shuffled down the gangplank across a stretch of heaving, filthy, menacing water. As Geordie pulled a handkerchief from his duffel coat pocket, a rubber toy flew out and fell fifty feet into the oily sea below. It was his Esso Man, a gift he had received a week earlier for his birthday. He didn't want to make a fuss so pretended he hadn't seen it fall.

A kindly Jamaican man tapped his grandmother on the shoulder and said, 'Your little boy has lost his toy in the water. Here, Ma'am – please take this.' He proffered a wrinkled ten-shilling note.

'Oh, you're so kind, but I couldn't possibly…'

'That's all right, Granny,' Geordie chipped in. 'He's happy in the water. Esso Man wants to go back to France. He'll jump on the next ferry and be there tomorrow.'

The Grange Primary School was run by Miss Godley-Brown in a handsome Victorian sandstone villa set in substantial gardens in Morningside. There were sixty children, of whom fifteen were boarders. The boarders were from Poland, Nigeria, England, Shetland and now Paris. It was a happy school where they learned to read, write, do basic sums and say their prayers every night and in the mornings. Table manners were all-important and the children were always impeccably turned out when they walked, crocodile fashion, to St John's Episcopal Church on the corner of Princes Street for the Sunday morning service.

Geordie was confused about the events that had overwhelmed his life. He was plucked from his kindergarten in Paris, forced to leave his ginger dog Nick, his beloved nanny Regine and his magic garden, then picked up and dumped in Edinburgh. His English had a distinct French accent and, despite making warm friends with the Polish boy and the Easton twins from Lagos, he was a lonely and rootless soul. When he lay in bed after lights-out he wondered where his mother was, what his father was doing, whether he would ever see his brother again. He wondered why he was there and who would take him out at half term. All the other children knew where they were going for the holidays. He received postcards every week from his mother in Montevideo, Addis Ababa, Geneva – an exotic array of places he could not even imagine. She seemed to be having a nice time. He rarely heard from his father and never from his brother.

At half-term people called Uncle Ian and Auntie Barbara came to take him out for the day. They went to see a film and he was returned to the school for the night, the only boarder left for the weekend. He developed a pain in his legs and strange rashes appeared. He heard Nurse Macmillan conferring with the doctor in hushed tones. Nurse didn't think it was serious but she thought it might be psychosomatic.

Geordie was moved to the Zoo, which was the name they gave to the san. He was the only child left in the school, alone in the Zoo. Nurse lived at the far end of the building and as he lay in bed he heard the pipes whooshing water around the central heating system. From the bowels of the building he heard a bell chime two times. The lights were out in the entire building. His only light was the orange glow from a street lamp on the other side of a huge lime tree. As the wind blew it threw patterns on the wall of the Zoo. Whoosh–whoosh of pipes, wind blowing, flickering orange shapes on the wall. Was that a goblin he saw? He shouted for Nurse. The bell chimed three times.

He hid under the covers. He slipped off to sleep and awoke in a nightmare. His boat was on fire and the house was ablaze. He was soaking with sweat. The bell chimed six times. Whoosh–whoosh, the wind blew. He lay in terror as the world burned around him. Orange flames licked at the wall, the boat was smoking. Was that a goblin laughing?

Nurse Macmillan shook the crumpled pile of sodden bedclothes. 'Time to get up, Geordie. I'll take your temperature and you can have some breakfast. Did you sleep well?'

A little voice replied, 'I'm not feeling very well. I don't know anybody.'

'You'll feel much better after breakfast. Doctor is coming this afternoon and I'm sure you'll be able to get up today and play.'

Geordie's leg pains were a mystery to the medical profession, but he knew what it was and told his friends that he had psychosomatic. He was the only boy at the school who had ever had this illness, which attracted admiration from the other children. They were careful with him at break times and on the playground. He was popular because he bore his pain with such panache.

One morning a tiny girl arrived as a day pupil at the school. Her name was Amo. They were told she was Egyptian and her father was a professor of medicine at Edinburgh University. She was brought into school by her mother, a trim, pretty lady with a nice smile for all the children she met at the school. Amo did not speak English and Miss Godley-Brown announced at prayers that everyone had to keep a close watch on her and make sure that she could keep up with lessons and on the playground. She then talked about Egypt, the pyramids and the pharaohs, and said how lucky they were to have little Amo at this school from such an ancient culture.

After considerable initial curiosity from the other children, Amo was soon ignored. She hung around the teachers at playtime because the other children were too busy chasing each other around the playground. Amo was too small and silent for the games. Geordie liked her. He imagined she was his little sister and even though there was nothing they could talk about, they played happily in the sand-pit and chased around the shrubbery playing peekaboo. Whenever she saw him her eyes lit up. He was gentle and always tried to include her in games with the other children. If they were too rough or fast for her, he would detach himself from their games and play with her.

Every afternoon at four o'clock Amo's mother came to the school to collect her and walk home. She got to know Geordie and would smile at him as she came up the steps to the front hall where the day children were assembled to be picked up. Geordie often sat on the steps waiting for her, just to feel the warm smile of a mother and the excitement of someone with a home just around the corner.

Amo's mother was late one afternoon and all the other day children had gone home. Only Amo was left in the hall, wearing a ridiculously large navy blue mackintosh and an oversized brown satchel on her little back. Geordie helped her take them off and they contrived a mad hide-and-seek game in the classrooms up and down stairs. Her head bobbed around the desks and tables, ringlets of black hair bouncing as she ran from room to room looking for places to hide from Geordie. Her eyes sparkled like black jewels and she betrayed her hiding spot with an explosion of laughter whenever he got close.

Geordie had never seen Amo so crazy and even though they could barely communicate with words he loved the games they played. They dashed up and down the main staircase of the house, lit by an enormous stained glass window of John the Baptist. The evening sunlight shone through it and the waters of the river Jordan filled the hall with iridescent blues and greens, like an aquarium.

They were right at the top of the house when Nurse Macmillan called upstairs to announce that Amo's mother had arrived. They fled downstairs, led by Geordie screaming with glee to see who would get to the hall first, taking three steps at a time and crashing from landing to landing. Little Amo was just behind him and launched herself into her mother's arms from the first flight of steps in the hall. She just managed to catch her flying daughter.

'My goodness, Amo, you really *are* wild tonight. It's time to get your things on and walk home.'

Geordie watched as she put on her oversized mackintosh and satchel again. He had never seen his four-year-old Egyptian friend so animated. Then, tugging her mother like a puppy on a lead, she shouted, 'Bye-bye, Geordie,' and pulled her out of the door. The door closed with a click.

The hall fell silent and Geordie sat on the steps looking at the dying rays of the sun through John the Baptist. He was sad that he couldn't go home and he didn't know when he would next see his family.

Assembly was always at 8.45 in the morning in the main hall. The children radiated out in a semicircle from the door of Miss Godley-Brown's office, from which she and the other teachers came out and conducted morning prayers. They were always the same: it started with a hymn, accompanied by Miss Goodwin on the piano in the hall, followed by a prayer, a bible reading, an announcement, a final hymn and a blessing. All the day-children were supposed to be at the school in their classrooms by 8.30, when they would file in orderly fashion to the hall and take their places for assembly. Geordie did not see Amo as the kindergarten class filed in. She was sometimes late because her mother walked everywhere.

Miss Godley-Brown came out of her office looking unusually severe. She announced a hymn which was new to the children. It was a sad hymn about Jesus and small children. The bible reading was about Jesus returning from the dead and during the prayer Geordie thought he saw Miss Godley-Brown crying. She spoke again: 'I have something very sad to say. Last night on her way home, little Amo was hit by a car and killed. She was too excited and didn't listen to her mother and ran on to the road. It's a terrible tragedy, but a real lesson to all of you here. You must always pay attention to the traffic and do what you are told by grown-ups. The school will be sending some flowers to her poor mother and father.'

Geordie looked at his feet then at John the Baptist. When assembly was over he rushed to his dormitory, buried his face in a pillow and sobbed piteously. It was his fault. He had got her so worked up that she behaved more wildly than ever before. She always held her mother's hand obediently, but not yesterday. She was tugging, pulling, impatient to play. It was the first time in her life she had been like that. He killed her. *He killed her.*

Nurse Macmillan found the boy with his face in the pillow and sat on the bed beside him. She put her hand gently on his back.

'God has a special place in heaven for little children. Amo was a lovely wee girl and God called her up because she was so special. You made her very happy, Geordie, and you always made a place for her when the other children didn't. She will always remember that in Heaven. One day you'll meet her again and you'll laugh and play with her for ever.'

His tear-streaked face pulled away from the pillow and he hugged Nurse Macmillan for a long time. 'Where's Montevideo?' was all he could think of saying.

Buzz

to Tom Gilbart

The boy had been leaning on the sill of his open bedroom window for a long time, abstractedly watching rooks circling above the grove of Scots pines at the end of the garden. By the time he heard the creak of footsteps on the landing outside his room it was too late, so he made no attempt to run back to his bed. His grandmother pushed the door open gently, expecting to see him asleep, and jumped when she saw him kneeling by the window.

'Goodness, Geordie, you gave me such a fright.'

The boy grinned.

'What on earth are you doing up so late?'

'Can't sleep.'

'Why not?'

'Don't know – just can't.'

She put her arms around her eleven-year-old grandson and both fell silent as together they observed the noisy spectacle of rooks cawing in the fading evening summer light.

'Granny?'

'Yes ?'

'What's it like being taught by a man?'

'Oh, not much different from a woman. Why?'

'Next term I'm going to be taught Latin by Buzz. I've only ever had lady teachers. The senior boys say he's ferocious and shouts and hits them if they make mistakes.'

'Nonsense – Buzz is a lovely man. I'm quite sure he's strict, but you'll learn a lot of Latin that way.'

'Well, Mrs Peacock was strict and sometimes whacked me, but what if Buzz whacks me? I've never been hit by a man.'

'Geordie, you're in the middle of your summer holidays and you're worrying about being taught by the best teacher in your school. It's way past your bedtime. Get into bed and we'll talk about it in the morning, when you're a bit more rational.'

'What's rational?'

'It's the best time to talk about things.'

'All right – we'll be rational in the morning.'

A month passed and the subject was not raised again. The first night at school was always hard. Boys were uncharacteristically silent and kept their own counsel when friends or teachers tried to engage them. They wanted to savour the last glow of warmth and domestic affection before the rowdy routine of a prep school normalized them into rough, tough little men.

Geordie's silence was deeper than usual because he dreaded encountering Buzz in the classroom the next morning. His friend Derek had gained confidence over the summer and tried to coax him into being more jolly.

'I'm not in the slightest scared of Buzz.' Derek hazarded to bring up the subject which had been on Geordie's mind all summer.

'Why's that, Derry?' Geordie affected casual interest.

'Because I'm going to tell my Dad if Buzz hits me. Dad'll beat the lights out of Buzz at half-term, tell the police and take me away from the school.'

'Can I sit behind you then?'

'No – you sit in the A to E row. I'm in the K to O row. You know that.'

'I really hope Buzz hits you: then we'll see your dad clobbering him at half-term. Will it be a straight smack in the chops, or a kick in the nuts?'

'Dad said he'd knock Buzz's lights out. That's all.'

'Well, that's something to look forward to.' Geordie chuckled.

Their first class in the morning was with Mrs Rickerby, who helped get them organized for the term. She was a big homely woman who regularly invited boys to tea with her family and was thoroughly nice, even though she was a lousy French teacher.

It was the second period they all dreaded.

Sixteen hearts stopped beating when the bell rang. They were set a French exercise for the next day and Mrs Rickerby left. The room was as tense as a tropical forest before a thunderstorm. They heard Buzz's characteristic humming approach along the corridor, interspersed with snatches from *Jerusalem* and *Why was 'e Born so Beautiful?* Slippers shuffled on the shiny linoleum, the brass doorknob turned and he entered. There was utter silence in the room as the wounded veteran of the Battle of Britain limped to the front of the class.

'Good morning, boys.'

Silence.

'I said, "GOOD MORNING, BOYS".'

'GOOD MORNING, SIR.'

'That's better.'

He picked out a long piece of white chalk from the wooden groove at the base of the blackboard. He placed the chalk on the master's desk and pulled a knotted rope from his worn tweed jacket. With a smile he held up the rope in view of the puzzled boys. Then with shocking ferocity he brought it crashing down on the chalk. It was pulverized in an explosion of splinters and dust.

Sixteen boys jumped from their seats and gave out a collective yelp.

'Any questions?' Buzz surveyed his cowed pupils.

'No? Good. Now let me tell you what I expect from a boy.'

Sixteen pairs of eyes swivelled simultaneously as Buzz paced the classroom, limping like a wounded tiger.

'CHARACTER.' The word rang in the chalky room.

'*Character* is the boy who persists when lesser boys crumple and sulk. *Character* is the rugby forward who gets hurt and keeps going. *Character* is the Spitfire pilot who could have baled out but who stayed with his burning machine to steer it away from a hospital. I expect no less from you.'

Sixteen boys nodded that they understood Buzz's definition of character.

'We have a lot to cover. We will begin by translating Caesar's *Gallic Wars* into the Queen's English, then translate your efforts back into Caesarean Latin. You will be marked for accuracy and purity of style. When I give you a passage to learn you will learn it thoroughly. In class we will proceed at random. I will point to one boy and tell him to give his translation of three lines. I will point to another boy and he will continue with the next three lines. We will study Caesar line by line at random around the classroom, so you will not get away with learning "your" lines and go to sleep. By the end of term you will know enough Latin to be exhibition scholars at Westminster. Any questions?'

Derek of the pugilist father put up his hand.

'Yes, boy?'

'Oh – it's nothing, Sir.'

'YES, boy?'

'Well, um, I was just going to ask… well, what if we finish Caesar before the end of term?'

'What's your name, boy?'

'Derek, Sir.'

'"Your NAME", I said.'

'Er, Derek Mikros, Sir.'

'Mikros ... Greek, eh?'

'Yes Sir – er, at least my grandfather was.'

'Mikros, you will see me after class and I will give you a short passage to recite to the class first thing tomorrow morning. I hate the thought of you being bored because Caesar is so easy.'

'Yes, Sir.'

The *Gallic Wars* were duly distributed and a passage for translation delineated for the next day. Mikros was given lines 45 to 49 of Virgil's *Aeneid* Book II to recite to the class in the morning. The lesson ended with a collective 'Phew' as the old man shuffled out. The boys turned to Mikros, who was close to tears.

'Cor. At least he didn't hit you, Derry.'

'What on earth were you thinking about? You were so cocky.' Geordie couldn't understand what possessed him to tempt the old man's wrath.

'I hate Buzz. I'll get him – you wait.'

'It would be a lot easier just to be quiet and do what he tells us, Derry. Learn your *Aeneid* for tomorrow and keep your head low for the rest of term, if you ask me.'

By the end of morning break the whole school was buzzing, at it were, with Mikros's daredevil stunt in the Latin class. Most boys thought he was a bloody fool, but could not help but be mightily impressed by his bravery.

The next morning at 9.45 Mikros was on the podium in front of the class. Buzz was staring out of the window, hands behind his back, fingers fidgeting.

'I like to start the day with poetry – don't you, Mikros? Before you start, I'm sure you learned the five lines I gave you yesterday?'

'Yes, Sir.'

'To save everybody time, I just want you to recite the final line I gave you.'

'Yes, Sir – er… *"Quicquid id est, timeo Danaos et dona ferentes".*'

Buzz was immobile for a long time before he spoke. 'Excellent, Mikros. Do you know what it means?'

'Er, not exactly, Sir.'

'It means, *"Whatever it is, I fear the Greeks – especially when bearing gifts".* This passage describes the arrival of a wooden horse outside the walls of Troy and the discussions held by the City elders as to what they should do with the horse. We all know what happened next – don't we, Mikros?'

'Yes, Sir.'

'Very good, Mikros. You can sit down now.'

Over the following weeks the class ploughed through the *Gallic Wars*. The fear driven into them at the start of term ensured faultless learning. Although he was a reasonable scholar and had no further scrapes with Buzz, Mikros was still determined to get revenge. An opportunity presented itself one Saturday afternoon during Scouts.

'Yikes! There's a snake – run for your lives!' Seven boys ran screaming out of their Scout camp on the edge of the woods. A brown snake was coiled on a low mossy rock in the autumn sun. It was a large female adder with a light brown zigzag pattern camouflaging her remarkably well in the autumn foliage. The Scoutmaster came striding into the camp to see what the fuss was all about. He saw the brown serpent and announced, 'Right, we'll close Blue Camp until winter, when adders hibernate.'

'Why don't you kill it, Sir?'

'Absolutely not. They won't harm you unless you threaten them or corner them. They don't like to be near humans. They're as entitled to live as you are.'

Mikros heard the kerfuffle from a neighbouring camp. After Scouts as it was getting dark he went furtively to Blue Camp to inspect the snake for himself. Sure enough, she remained coiled on the moss. She stirred and raised her head towards him, but he was quicker. With thick leather gloves he flicked her into a black garden polythene bag and held the neck tightly. The snake writhed at the bottom and Mikros carried his prize gingerly to the bicycle shed, where he knew nobody would come until the next morning. He made a few pin-pricks in the bag and hung it by the neck from a wooden rafter.

At supper that evening Buzz was at the top table chatting with other masters and some prefects. He announced that he was going fishing at the local reservoir next morning after church. Buzz loved fishing. He would typically pack up his gear and sandwiches in a khaki army knapsack before church and make a quick departure by bicycle to the reservoir. He would be gone for a few hours, then return in time for evensong, usually with a trout or two for dinner.

After supper Mikros cornered his friend. 'Hey Geordie, I have an idea. You remember I'm a Catholic?'

'Well, yes', Geordie was accustomed to Mikros's flights of fancy and wondered where this one was going.

'You know I don't have to go to church with the school on Sunday mornings?'

'Well?'

'Come with me. Keep your voice down,' he whispered.

Mikros led Geordie outside the main building towards the bicycle shed. It was dark but he had a small pen torch. They clambered over a few bikes and he shone the torch on a black polythene bag hanging from the rafters.

'What's that?'

'The snake. From Blue Camp this afternoon.'

'Blimey. What are you doing with that?' They were already doubly out of bounds: outside after dark, and in the bicycle shed. Now Geordie was getting seriously afraid.

Mikros cupped the bottom of the black bag with his gloved hands. There was a faint movement in the shiny polythene.

A door banged behind the bicycle shed. The boys froze. There was no further sound. 'Must have been the wind,' Geordie whispered hopefully.

Mikros shook the bag. 'I'm going to put it in Buzz's knapsack. It'll be furious when it's released and it'll bite Buzz. I hope it kills him. It'll slide away and nobody will know it wasn't an accident.'

'I think you're mad. You mustn't do that.'

'You hate Buzz, too – you've told me so. You're part of my plan now.'

'I don't hate him that much any more. I don't want to kill him and nor should you. Your Latin is quite good now. You even got an alpha last week.'

'When everyone's in church I'll go to Buzz's room and put the snake in his knapsack.'

'I don't want anything to do with it. I'm going to tell a prefect.'

'If you tell, after Buzz dies I'll find a way to kill you too. Anyway, nobody will believe you. I'm going to move the snake and nobody'll find it. Now scoot back to the house before I get you.' He shook the bag and shone the torch on the squirming black plastic.

Geordie ran madly in the dark back to the house. He couldn't believe that Mikros would do what he said. Later in the dormitory as they went to bed Mikros caught his eye and gestured with a finger across the throat.

He hardly slept that night. Several times he tried to get up and steal out to the nurse's room to tell her. Mikros was in the doorway before him, brandishing the blade of a penknife at his stomach.

'Get back into bed, Geordie. I wish I hadn't told you.'

'I wish you hadn't either.'

It was the longest Sunday in Geordie's life. He avoided Mikros but was aware of being shadowed by the boy. Whenever he got close to a master or a prefect Mikros was there first.

'Derry, leave me alone,' was all he managed to say to his shadow, who smiled back in a weirdly menacing way.

It was a tremendous relief when Geordie saw Buzz returning on his bicycle that evening, as usual. He carried a brown trout in a net and whistled *Danny Boy* as he rode up the drive. Mikros looked baffled, then completely deflated. The usual crowd of boys surrounded Buzz to inspect his catch and everything seemed absolutely normal.

'It must have got out. That's just as well. You shouldn't try that again.'

'Shut up, Geordie. Just shut up.'

'I will. I don't ever want to be your friend again.'

On Monday Latin was the first lesson of the day. As usual the boys sat with folded hands on their desks when Buzz entered the room. He tested them verbally on the Caesar they had learned the previous week, then told them to get their books out of their desks. There was a scream. Mikros recoiled and knocked his chair backwards. A writhing brown snake had its fangs embedded in the soft tissue of his right hand. Buzz took out his knotted rope and with a well-aimed crack, hit the snake hard. It fell to the wooden floor, lifeless.

He pulled Geordie roughly out of his seat. 'You'd better get Mikros to the nurse quickly.'

Geordie put his arm around his whimpering friend's shoulder and steered him out of the classroom towards the infirmary. As they went past him Buzz smiled thinly and muttered to Mikros, ' *"Quicquid id est, timeo Danaos et dona ferentes".*'

He picked the hapless viper off the floor and dropped it into the wastepaper-bin. Addressing the class he resumed the lesson. 'Settle down, boys. We have work to do. Now turn to page 34 of *De Bello Gallico.*'

The Platform

to Bobby Lachman and Benedicte
for a truly golden summer

Geordie wrote to his father in Paris to say he couldn't visit that summer because he was committed to his mother's plans until the end of August. He wrote to his mother saying that he needed to improve his French and would be spending the summer in Paris with his father. His father wrote back, ostensibly sad but actually quite relieved that his son wouldn't be interfering with his routine in Paris. His mother wrote back, actually sad but sympathetic to the need of her son to improve his French. His parents had not spoken for five years so he reckoned his subterfuge was foolproof.

He then informed his wealthy classmates who, for years, had said casually, 'If you're ever in the South of France, my man, look us up'. They rapidly back-pedalled when their school friend unwittingly called their bluff and actually intended to stay on their non-existent yachts in Antibes and Cannes. Boats suddenly steamed off to Tangiers, were engaged on long-term charter in the Pelopponese or inexplicably required by Hollywood friends in the Virgin Islands.

Geordie was not put off. He managed to glean a few hard addresses and booked his ticket to the Côte d'Azur. On the way he spent a few days in London dossing down with friends.

That summer London was swarming with shoeless boys and girls from the best schools. They gathered in parks and flats smoking dope with flowers in their hair listening to Sergeant Pepper and Procol Harum, desperately jostling from place to place in the attempt to be Where It's At. Geordie was part of this shifting tide of privileged flotsam, so the idea of travelling alone around Europe for the summer with one overnight bag seemed quite in keeping with the prevailing culture.

He left Victoria station early one morning and settled down for the long journey to the south of France. He changed stations in Paris and boarded a train for Nice. After Lyons the scenery changed subtly from the damp green maritime plains of northern Europe to the hazy shimmering vista of dry limestone hills of central France. His carriage was filled with French soldiers. They slid open the windows and hung out in the train's slipstream. Warm southern air billowed through the carriage. Geordie caught the passing scent of lavender fields, mown hay and garlic and was transfixed by the vineyards of the Rhône Valley. He was in a dream of anticipation. Sixteen years old, six weeks of time, single and free.

Late the next afternoon Geordie got off at St Raphaël. He called his friend Dominic and was told to take the bus to St Tropez from the *arrêt* in front of the station. He exited into an ochre-tinted square which glowed like firebricks in the evening sun. An elderly charabanc marked *Ste Maxime, St Tropez* waited at the stop and he clambered aboard.

The bus ride along the coast was slow and magical. Everyone Geordie saw was bronzed and relaxed. He relished the glorious mixture of scents of Ambre Solaire, cooking herbs and the Mediterranean. The girls were stylish, sexy and tanned. He felt conspicuously British and un-cool in his Viyella shirt and flannel trousers.

Dominic met him off the bus in the family's battered Citroen 2CV, sheepishly warning him, 'My aunt isn't very well, so I'm afraid you can only stay two, maybe three, nights. After that you'll have to fend for yourself.'

Geordie was taken aback, but played cool. He had expected to stay for ten days, orient himself, then play the gypsy. They drove a few miles past St Tropez and turned into a rough drive flanked by date palms. The car stopped in the courtyard of a rambling Provençal farmhouse. A hint of wood smoke hung in the still air and cicadas hissed in the trees. Geordie was led through to a veranda lit by hurricane-lamps and candles. Eight people in various stages of stupefaction were lounging around in wicker chairs and couches. They were an older crowd, well over 30.

'*Je veux vous présenter à mon ami, Geordie, d'origine Ecosse.*'

A man with a tanned wrinkled face and curled blond locks leered at him. He spoke English in the manner of BBC announcers in the 1950s, 'How do you do, Geordie. My name is Poulos.' Geordie shook his hand, which showed little inclination of letting go.

An elderly woman covered incongruously with a rug held out her hand. 'I take it that Dom told you about my health. We simply cannot entertain guests with my hip the way it is.'

'Yes, he told me. I quite understand.'

She looked at least forty and clearly this was not an illness that had come along overnight. Geordie wished he'd been told earlier. He now had a serious gap in his plans.

'Very well, then. Perhaps you could make arrangements to be on your way by Saturday.'

'Er... yes, that's no problem. I appreciate you having me to stay here.' He smiled unconvincingly at the woman and looked hard at Dominic, who averted his gaze and continued introducing him around the group. Here was a famous pre-war opera singer, there a Greek prince, here a poetess from Paris. 'You remind me of Rimbaud as a young man. Do you write poetry?'

'Sometimes.'

Dominic was a lonely boy incarcerated with an effete group of faded celebrities for the summer. The house was old, the people were old. Even their French bulldog Bouboule was ancient, hissing gas under a chaise longue. This was a far cry from his boasting at school. Where was the stereo booming out the Beach Boys and Rolling Stones? Where was his motor bike? Where were the beautiful girls? The cabinet full of Bacardi?

Geordie was not offered anything to eat or drink, so after a polite interval he announced he was tired and wouldn't mind hitting the hay. He was shown a lumpy couch in the diningroom beside a swing door to the kitchen. He unfurled his sleeping bag and tossed it on the couch. Nobody was around, so he grabbed the heel of a baguette and a peach off the kitchen table. He took a large swig of Vichy water and vanished into a cloakroom to wash. He looked at the tousled, grimy youth in the mirror. It was Wednesday night in the south of France and he had not changed clothes since Tuesday morning in London.

'No wonder they want me out of here,' he laughed. 'You've arrived in a fine spot here, matey. Go to St Tropez in the morning, scout it out. You need to move quickly.'

It was clear that the couch represented the limit of hospitality he could expect. He would have to ghost his way around the house, using the bathroom before anyone got up, stealing scraps from the kitchen and ensuring that his traces were cleared from the dining area before breakfast – to which he had not been invited.

It was an uncomfortable predicament for any 16-year-old. He awoke early on the first morning and lay on the couch until the first streaks of light appeared outside. He had to confront Dominic and find out what was going on. Fortunately Dom had pointed out his room as they walked through the house the previous evening: it had a Haight-Ashbury sticker on the door. Geordie fumbled down the badly-lit passage and found it.

'Dominic, it's me, Geordie.' He flicked on the light and shook his friend.

'What's going on, man?' Somewhere under the boy's thick black hair was a face.

'Dominic, I need to know what's happening. Your aunt wasn't expecting me, was she?'

'Man, I didn't think you'd show up so I didn't tell her. These things are normally arranged parent to parent, so it seems weird to her that a boy would just show up. Bad form. That's what she said.'

'OK, Dom. It's all been a screw-up. Can you take me into St Tropez this morning? I want to get some decent clothes and look around.'

'Sure – only I don't have the car today. Take my bike. It's in the courtyard. St Tropez is only three miles from here.'

'So you can't come with me?'

'I need to hang out here.' Dominic sat propped up by a pillow in bed, looking peevish.

Geordie returned to his room and bundled his belongings out of sight under the couch. He slipped his journal into a back pocket, took another peach from the kitchen and pointed the bike towards St Tropez.

The only animation in the town at seven in the morning was provided by café proprietors hosing Gauloise stubs and food scraps off the pavement into the gutter. Boats sat at anchor in the glassy water; a small dog was peeing against the railing on a Panama-registered cruiser, leaving a yellow streak down the pristine white paintwork of the million-dollar boat.

Geordie sat at a nearby café, ordered breakfast and began writing his journal. He was completely absorbed when he heard a man's voice, '*Eh bien, jeune homme, comment ça va?* A middle-aged faggot had sidled up to the next table and began to chat in French. Geordie affected complete ignorance, but the man spotted his writing and switched to impeccable English. He was Belgian, an artist and apparently world famous. He had a portfolio with him and proceeded to show lewd prints of the worst sort. 'These are in many famous collections.' He showed articles from the *International Herald Tribune*, *New York Times* and *Le Figaro*, comparing his work to Braque and Picasso.

'I invite you to see my studio. Bobby Darin bought some of my work.'

'I'm not in the market for fine art. Now piss off and let me finish my breakfast in peace.'

The man wasn't accustomed to such words from his prospective young victims. He tried to raise the stakes for the handsome British boy, flagged the waiter and ordered two coffees and a basket of bakeries, but Geordie got up and left the café.

He found a beach and stretched out in the morning sun. When he woke up much later, parasols and towels were spread around him. A French girl with black hair and sparkling brown eyes lay on a mat four feet from his face. She wore only the bottom section of a bikini. She was with another girl and they were giggling at him. He sat up, shaking sand from his hair and clothes. He wore the same Viyella shirt and grey flannel trousers he had worn for days. Not only did it look bizarre on a beach in St Tropez but he smelled like a polecat. He smiled sheepishly and shrugged.

'*J'ai perdu ma valise*,' was all he could say, which the girls found hilarious. They talked more. The topless one was called Christianne. She lent him a towel and pointed him towards a shower cubicle at the beach. Then she would take him shopping.

Long after dark he steered his bicycle back from St Tropez and bumped down the pitted palm-lined track towards the old farmhouse. Lights were still on and he heard the hum of conversation on the back veranda. He was in such a good mood that he felt able to face them and walked over. Dominic rose to head him off but his aunt got in first. 'Young man, I am disgusted by your behaviour. You are here as my guest and not only did you disappear without saying where you were going but visitors who stay here are expected to fall in with the family. How are we supposed to cater for people who don't show up for meals?'

Geordie was flushed with the fragrance of Christianne and this old crone in a blanket was a travesty of his expectations of the south of France. Without hesitation, he replied, 'The first thing you made clear when I arrived last night was that I was unwelcome. I came in after a long journey from London and wasn't even offered a glass of water, let alone something to eat. Stop pretending that you care about your guests. I agreed to leave on Saturday, but if you will permit me to spend one more night here I'll be happy to leave tomorrow morning.'

Turning to his friend he added, 'Dominic, I'm sorry. You invited me for ten days and the place you described was completely different from this. I'm sorry I came. Goodnight.'

There was an embarrassed silence as Geordie angrily retreated from the veranda. When he lay on the couch he thought of the wonderful things that had happened that day. He drifted off and slept deeply until he was awakened by Dominic at seven the next morning.

'Hey Geordie, what are your plans?'

'Leave here as soon as possible, preferably without seeing your aunt. I'll go into St Tropez to say goodbye to Christianne, then hitch up the coast towards Cannes.'

'Who's Christianne?'

Geordie told him.

Dominic fell silent. His friend from school had met a girl on his first day in St Tropez. He'd been there all summer and knew nobody of his own age.

Geordie showered, put on his new baggy khaki trousers and loose Egyptian cotton shirt, slipped on a pair of espadrilles, swung the tote bag around his shoulder and stood to attention, quite the hippy.

'OK, pal, let's hit the road.' He handed an envelope to Dominic. 'It's a thank you letter for your aunt. Got to maintain protocol, don't you know.'

Dominic drove him to St Tropez. As he got out of the vehicle, Geordie was not feeling charitable. 'Thanks, mate. I realize you're in a difficult situation and I won't say anything at school. But do yourself a favour and shut up about the playboy lifestyle you lead. I've had more fun staying with friends in Doncaster than with you on the Côte d'Azur. See you back at school in September.' He left his glum friend to mosey back to his aunt's farmhouse.

Geordie made his way through the narrow streets and found the little boutique where Christianne worked. He sat in the café opposite nursing a glass of *pastis* and wrote his journal while he waited for the boutique to open.

'...A brief stay near St Tropez. Accommodation turned out to be non-existent so I'm heading up the coast to see what Brian, Patrick and the others are up to. I met a lovely girl on the beach yesterday called Christianne. She showed me around the place. She took me to a boutique where she got the guy to use me to model some clothes, which they gave me as "used". I got a pair of khaki trousers, a white cotton shirt and some espadrilles for *nothing*. I chucked my old clothes into a bin by the harbour. I'm now dressed for the south of France.

'She took me to her mother's flat. Strict Catholics, nicely brought up. We were sitting in a café with her friends and my French ran out. I tried to listen to their conversation, mostly in the Provençale argot, which washed right over me – so I looked her in the eye after my third *pastis* and kissed her. Her friends were paired off too so it seemed right... we spent the evening together and mooched about St Tropez.

'I would love to stay with her but her mother wouldn't let it happen. So I'll say goodbye and hitch up the coast...'

He saw her opening the boutique across the road. She was as cute as a doll with a shining black ponytail. She wore a short white cotton dress and the tone of her brown legs was set off stunningly by red high-heeled shoes. She smelled of a light breezy perfume. He tried to explain his situation. It was very much his intention to come back but she seemed disappointed.

He walked for two miles along the dusty road towards Ste Maxime, found a suitable place on the roadside and stood with his thumb in the air. It took six rides and eight hours to reach Cannes, a distance of about sixty kilometres. The French were notoriously mean to hitch hikers: evidently a favourite pastime was to stop a hundred metres ahead, wait for them to reach the car with their bags in the heat, then accelerate off, leaving them in a shower of gravel and abuse by the side of the road.

In Cannes he went straight to the marina to search for his friend Brian's cruiser, *Baby Blue*. He paced every berth in the Marina but there was no boat by that name. He called the phone number Brian gave him: '*hors de service*'.

Eventually he found an employee at the marina who informed him that *Baby Blue* had not been at Cannes for at least three years. As far as he knew it was on charter in the Caribbean.

'Another bullshitter,' exclaimed Geordie.

It was late afternoon and he needed a place to stay. Cannes was not sympathetic to down-and-outs. Everyone else seemed connected, paired off, in company. Waiters in white coats served couples at glitzy cocktail bars in front of fabulously affluent hotels. He caught sight of himself in the plate glass of a shop and he looked good: a tall, slender blond boy in light summer clothes. He had caught the sun and his hair bleached easily. At least he didn't look like a bum. He caught the eye of some girls and felt himself mentally stripped as he passed well-dressed gentlemen sitting alone at expensive watering places.

Most of the beach front was allocated to hotels which demanded an extortionate price to enter the sea over cordoned ground. There didn't seem to be a public beach. It was late afternoon and the flow of people was away from the shore. Beach boys everywhere were busy folding up parasols and deck chairs.

In the mêlée Geordie walked into the most exclusive enclosure he could find, stripped to his underpants, threw his stuff on an empty deck chair and ran into the warm Mediterranean. He swam vigorously for half an hour. When he came out he walked confidently to a cubicle and took a long fresh shower using the hotel's best soap and shampoo. He used their fluffy freshly laundered towels to dry off.

His clothes and tote bag were still on the deck chair. He picked them up, returned to the cubicle, changed and strolled confidently out of the compound.

'Now I can face the night,' he thought. The smell of *bouillabaisse* and expensive cooking wafted along the promenade. Girls were dressed for the evening, everyone in Cannes seemed utterly relaxed after a day in the sun, a shower, and as often as not, he imagined, a good tumble in a shaded room. Geordie was clean and respectable, but felt isolated. Fragrant young girls brushed past him whispering, *'Cinquante francs, plus la chambre'* – fifty francs, plus the room – but he didn't have the fifty francs or a room to offer.

He wandered inland to the cheap accommodation zone. Every

hostel was full. He found a park where he staked a place on a bench. As the evening wore on he wondered why benches were so popular with down-and-outs. They were not comfortable. They were draughty and were an obvious target for robbers, sexual predators or worst of all, the police.

Two well-spoken English teenagers were stretched out on the bench next to his, but didn't see the humour of their predicament. They had come to the South of France 'For one thing, really – sex.' They hadn't found it, but did discover the taste of homelessness and loneliness on their voyage. The hallowed halls of Haileybury and Bradfield hadn't prepared them for this kind of life. He didn't catch their names, so thought of them as Hailey and Brad. Geordie felt better equipped for this experience than his southern counterparts. Sleeping on a park bench in Cannes in July was certainly no worse than a Duke of Edinburgh's Award hike up a Scottish mountain in March.

He rose at first light. Today his project was to find his friend, Patrick, whose family had a villa up the coast in Antibes. He had an address and a telephone number. He would call after breakfast and try his luck. As he rose he saw Hailey and Brad curled up in the same sleeping bag, asleep beside their bench. 'Looks like they found what they were looking for,' he thought.

He wandered back towards the beach, buying a kilo of fresh peaches and a litre of milk on the way. He found a long jetty underpinned by huge concrete blocks and strolled to the end. Here he decided to set out his breakfast with a view of the Cannes coastline, write his journal and plan the day. The soft early sun played on his back as he ate peach after peach, followed by gulps of milk. It didn't take long. His gut was overwhelmed by the invasion of foreign bacteria demanding an urgent exit. Geordie had about ten seconds to react, perched over a concrete block and let rip. A sleeping fisherman on the concrete below received the full blast of Geordie's outburst. A furious, stunned string of Arabic oaths rent the calm morning air as the man dived into the sea and swam vigorously away from the spot.

It took Geordie an hour to purge himself after which he felt less ambitious than when he rose that morning. He ambled slowly back along the jetty and dived into deep water closer to the shore to freshen up. He napped in the rising sunshine and was not ready to call Patrick until early afternoon. He found a phone booth and called the number.

The voice of a young girl answered, 'Oh, Patrique is in Paris, he won't be coming to Antibes this summer.'

'Did Patrick say that his friend Geordie Kinloch was coming to stay in Antibes?'

'Non.'

'Could I speak to your parents, please?'

'They're playing tennis and will be back after five o'clock.'

'Would you please tell them I called. Perhaps you could call Patrick in Paris too, tell him I called and would like to take up his invitation to stay in Antibes? I would be most grateful.'

He heard a low whistle at the other end, 'Oh là là, I don't sink my parents will like zis.'

'That's fine – I'll call back after five this afternoon. Thanks for your help. *Au revoir.*'

'*Au revoir.*'

'Three out of three,' he mused as he put the receiver back slowly on the hook. 'If only I had a roof over my head for a couple of nights I could begin to have a decent holiday down here.'

His grand plan for cruising the Med in his friends' yachts surrounded by lovely girls from rich families had degenerated into an amorphous, desperate strategy for surviving the next few days. He could always go home to a parent; his return ticket to London was in his top pocket. He decided to walk in the direction of Antibes, clear his mind and explore the coastline. If they couldn't take him, at least Antibes was a step closer to Monte Carlo, where he would try to track down Bobbie Spachter, the last of his school friends with an open invitation. If that failed, he had a friend in Rome…

Geordie walked slowly in the heat through Juan les Pins. The cicadas in the scented pines gave out their lazy hissing sound, the eternal Mediterranean accompaniment to splashing pools and making love. The unspoken affluence and his sense of exclusion were stifling. For the first time in his life he felt completely outside, irrelevant, isolated. At 5.30 he picked up a phone in a café in Antibes and dialled Patrick's parents. A sharp English female voice answered, 'Hell-e-o?'

'Yes, hello. I'm Geordie Kinloch, a school friend of Patrick's. He said that if I was ever in the area I should call.'

'How very nice of you. We'll tell him you called.'

'He won't be around this week?'

'He won't be around this summer.'

'Er, well, tell him I'm sorry to have missed him.'

'Yes. I expect he will be sorry to have missed you.'

'Well, goodbye then.'

Geordie hung up and banged his head on the phone booth wall. 'Damn, what a bitch. She knew exactly why I was calling and let me twist in the air. What kind of people are these friends of mine?'

Six o'clock and another park bench beckoned. A bus to Nice was waiting just outside the café so he made the snap decision to jump on board. Half an hour later he was walking along the promenade in Nice. The beach had plenty of public access. He decided to set up his sleeping bag under the boardwalk and join a multitude of hippies doing the same thing. A group of American and English girls lay stretched on blanket along the beach from him. One Canadian called himself 'The Bear', after his resemblance to the lead singer from Canned Heat. There was nothing hard-core about them, just gentle, aimless people drifting through their vacations, enjoying Hippy brotherhood. Geordie was glad to attach himself to these people. He felt safe as sleep washed over him and the sound of waves on the pebbles receded from his consciousness.

He woke up to total pandemonium. He didn't know where he was or what was happening. It was pitch-dark, searchlights flashed on and off. A klaxon sounded incessantly and someone was directing a powerful hose at him. He was blown in the air by a jet of water and pushed against the lower concrete wall of the boardwalk. He couldn't move under the intense power of the water, then it dropped him and did the same to a Dutch couple near him. They were washed ten yards along the beach.

'Some bastard's got a great sense of humour,' he thought as he pulled himself together on the shingle.

The hoses and klaxons stopped. A searchlight remained trained on the sodden heaps of humanity which ten minutes earlier were sleeping harmlessly. A voice came over on a bull horn, *'C'est la Police. Il est absolument défendu de se coucher sur la plage. On vous donne dix minutes de quitter la plage.'*

A naked long-haired man walked towards the bullhorn and was struck down by the police. He was left groaning where he fell. The Bear shouted out, 'This is war – but they've got all the weapons, and they're lookin' for a fight. Keep calm. Do exactly as they say and get off the beach. Don't resist, keep cool.'

A bedraggled line of hippies stumbled over the shingle on to the promenade. It was 2.30 in the morning and they collapsed in confusion like refugees on benches and grass verges.

In the morning Geordie sat silently with the group of Canadians, stunned by the night's events. One of them said he'd heard of a place in a forest above Nice where 'kids were hanging out' and were left alone. Geordie said he would come with them to check it out. The hippies decamped from the beach area and hiked uphill along a pleasant road through suburbs and groves of Corsican pines. On the way they met a couple of English hippies, all beads and guitars. 'Man, follow us to the Platform. It's cool and there's plenty of space. It's a mile up the hill from here.'

They trudged to a large concrete platform built into a hillside overlooking the city. It was sheltered by pines and groups of people had laid out sleeping bags and tents in the shade. A tousled fair-haired English boy with a beardy stubble met them. 'Hi, I'm Jeremy. The fuzz leave us alone if we keep to the rules. If we break them they'll close the Platform down. Simple. The rules are: no pissing, shitting or littering around the Platform. Do that in town before you turn in for the night. If you're caught short in the middle of the night, run two hundred yards up the road and do it under a tree. No fires. The fuzz are paranoid about forest fires. No drugs. Don't run around naked. No weapons or fighting. No loud music.'

At that moment a shirtless boy who looked like James Dean roared up the road on a red 500cc Triumph and rolled onto the Platform. He stopped the front wheel beside Jeremy and cut the engine. A thin joint hung from the corner of his mouth. He pulled a newspaper from behind his belt and threw it at Jeremy. The French headline proclaimed a 'Successful clean up of foreign vermin from our beaches.'

'I met some folks who were hosed off the beach last night by the cops. When d'ya reckon they'll do it here? It says it took 200 CRS riot police to get the hippies under control. That's heavy, man.'

'That's total bullshit,' The Bear spoke up. 'We were asleep at the time and gave them no trouble at all. They turned fire hoses on us without provocation. We didn't resist. Show me the paper.' He took it from Jeremy and read aloud, 'Large groups of drug-taking hooligans provoked police by throwing rocks from the beach.' He laughed. 'That's a complete lie.'

Jeremy looked unconcerned. 'The police will leave us alone here if we keep to the rules. Sleeping on the beach irritates the hotels and the paying public. Here we're out of the way. Find yourselves a place on the Platform. We have about sixty people here every night. We eat, drink, smoke and rock together after dark. It's cool, man – but keep to the Rules, OK?'

Geordie was tired. He laid his sleeping bag on the concrete, stretched out and closed his eyes. He was wakened a couple of hours later by a pretty girl in a floral dress playing a guitar and singing Donovan's *Catch the Wind*. Geordie stared at the blue sky through the branches and breathed in the warm pine-scented air. Cicadas hissed in the trees. He belonged somewhere for the first time since he arrived on the Coast. He would stay awhile.

That evening they pooled a meal of French cheeses, vegetables, fruit, bread and wine. Guitars strummed, they danced and sang.

'This is pure communism, man,' an intense German purred knowingly.

'Shit, are they sending tanks now?' The Bear leaped off the platform in feigned terror and peered down the darkened road.

At that moment Geordie's two friends from Cannes arrived at the Platform. He got up unsteadily and shouted out, 'Hey, everybody, this is Hailey and Brad from England. Make room for them.' The boys were pleased to see a friendly face and space was made for them. Joints were rolled and passed around. Geordie turned into a beam of light and accelerated at warp speed into the night sky to the outer planets. He giggled uncontrollably; a bearded Swede played the banjo. Every note entered his brain, turned into colours and flew around like a rainbow with wings. He had never heard music like that.

Some of the group always agreed to stay during the day to keep an eye on the Platform. The others, relieved of their belongings, wandered down to the beach in Nice to swim, wash, explore and pick up more people. Every night there was a fresh crop of new talent to share the happenings on the Platform. Crazy poets, mime artists, musicians and actors passed through. The Platform became famous in the local cultural underground.

As the weeks passed it began to get squalid. Drugs were easily available, some hippies began to neglect themselves. Geordie noticed a difference. The hard drug crowd crossed a wall into another land. They were distant, self-absorbed and lost the communal spirit that pervaded the Platform a few weeks earlier. Jeremy and his girlfriend crossed over, as did two Canadians. James Dean crashed his Triumph and was airlifted to Frankfurt where he was repatriated to the USA in chains for deserting his unit in Vietnam. Hailey and Brad fell in with a hard gay crowd. Their eyes became cold and distant, the innocence of the Cannes park bench lost forever. The sweet flower power of July was turning into a dark August. Money, cameras and clothes were being stolen. The police were showing interest in the project. Trust was gone.

One morning Geordie pulled the last telephone number from his list and called Bobby Spachter. He got straight through.

'Man, I've been waiting for your call. Where are you?'

'In Nice.'

'Great. Come on over. Wanna stay a few days?'

'That would be brilliant. I warn you, though, I'm pretty scruffy. I've been living rough for a few weeks.'

'No sweat, man. We'll clean you up. Meet me in the lobby of the Hôtel de Paris at 12 noon today.'

Geordie raced back to the Platform and scooped up his tattered things. His clothes were ragged like a street person's. He could only guess how badly he smelled. He made some quick decisions. It was Monday. He would stretch his stay with Bobbie and catch a train to London on Friday or Saturday. He still had 200 francs in his inside pocket. He would buy one clean outfit, steal a shower on the beach in Nice and throw away his used clothes and the filthy tote bag. He would keep his wash things, camera, passport and money. Geordie's hippy phase ended at precisely that moment.

Bobby dressed in the way that very rich people thought hippies should dress. Tailored emerald flared corduroy trousers, black Italian loafers. A thick gold chain adorned his neck, a white silk shirt, a casually knotted printed silk foulard by Dior. He wore his hair in a bouffant style like Eric Clapton on the cover of *Disraeli Gears*, his sideburns were angled and he carried a whiff of Givenchy for Men. He took one look at Geordie and remarked, 'Man, you look like shit.'

Geordie felt awkward in the lobby of the Hôtel de Paris. 'Thanks, Bobby. So where are we going?'

'Upstairs.'

Bobby's parents took a suite at the Hôtel de Paris each summer.

Most of the time Bobby had the place to himself. The boys took the lift upstairs and Bobby pushed open a door. 'This is your room.'

It was flooded with sunshine, fabulously clean, modern, white, fragrant and comfortable. Light curtains billowed in the breeze coming off the Mediterranean.

'Bobby, you know where I've been these last few weeks? I've been sleeping rough around Nice. This is unimaginable luxury.'

'It's your room this week, my friend. Take a shower. There's the shampoo – don't spare the soap. Use one of these razors. Clean your nails, man – they're disgusting. When you're done we'll throw out your clothes and get some new ones brought in. I'll come back in an hour.' He headed out of a connecting door.

After a minute he stuck his head in the door again. He threw a room service menu at Geordie, who was still staring out at the harbour and pondering his surreal change of fortune. He caught the menu.

'Order yourself something off of this. You've lost weight. Ciao.' He disappeared again, slamming the door.

'Thanks, man.' Geordie surveyed the menu. Room service for the cheapest item cost more than he spent on food for a week on the Platform. He knew his friend was wealthy but he hesitated to exploit the situation. He ordered a modest burger with a glass of milk. He then dived into the shower where he stood in a jet of water for ten minutes, scrubbing every inch of his body. He washed his hair twice. The water draining off him was brown, even after his second full wash. Dirt from the Platform had clogged his pores and his skin had taken on the yellowish hue of the chronically homeless. He finished his scrub with a high-pressure cold shower, which left him tingling with energy.

The burger arrived on a gold trolley under a silver lid. There was a starched linen napkin, monogrammed cutlery, a side order of fries in a silver dish, dinky little pepper and salt shakers.

'What a load of shit this all is,' Geordie mused. He picked up the burger with his hands and bit off a huge mouthful. 'But damn, it tastes good.'

41

Bobby entered from the connecting door with a pretty, dark-haired woman carrying a pile of flat boxes. She put them on his bed.

'Geordie, this is Honey. She works at the Carnaby Boutique in Monte Carlo and has brought some clothes. I reckoned you were pretty much my size, a bit skinnier perhaps. I tried them on and they fit me, so they should be OK for you.'

'Hi, Honey.' Geordie was immediately taken by the petite French girl.

'Hi, Geordie. If anything needs to be altered I can get it done straight away.'

Honey opened the boxes and laid out the most lovely clothes a 16-year-old boy could imagine. A pair of pale blue flared corduroy trousers, two pairs of hand stitched calfskin loafers – one black, one brown – two white silk shirts, a white cotton shirt, a lightweight linen jacket, a pair of khaki flared trousers, baggy swimming trunks ('Gotta have these at the beach club, man,') and a selection of paisley patterned silk scarves.

'Put on the khakis and a white shirt for now. When we go out tonight you can put on the cords and the jacket.' Thus spake Bobby Spachter.

Geordie disappeared into the bathroom with an armful of new clothes and emerged looking quite the tanned, slim playboy. His hair had grown over the summer, bleached by the salt of his daily bath in the Mediterranean. The brown calfskin shoes slipped on as if tailored for him. He emerged from the bathroom with a Fred Astaire flourish – 'Ta-daa ....'

Honey straightened each garment and stepped back to admire her creation. '*Qu'il est beau, ce garçon .*'

'All right, you look great. Thanks, Honey. Let's head down to the Beach Club and see what's happening. We'll take all this stuff, Honey. Put it on my account.'

Of the four friends who invited Geordie to stay that summer, Bobby had been the most reticent. He simply invited him to stay if he came to Monte Carlo. There was no bragging: just, 'Come visit for a few days if you're around.' Geordie knew he was heir to a famous American fortune, but never imagined that anyone would have so much cash to play with at 16.

His chauffeur met them outside the lobby and drove them to the SBM Beach Club. They walked past piles of fresh towels and beach mattresses on which were stretched some of the prettiest girls Geordie had seen on the Côte d'Azur. They all knew Bobby and most spoke English with an American accent. He headed out along a jetty and waved. A shining teak and chrome Riva speedboat came gurgling up to the jetty, piloted by an Italian with wavy greasy backswept long hair and mirror sunglasses. He wore a Hawaiian shirt and baggy shorts.

'Carlo, this is my friend Geordie. I want you to take us to San Remo. I'll see if any of the girls want to come. He whistled from the jetty as for a dog. Two girls leapt off their beach chairs and came running down in their bikinis. One was tall, dark haired and slim. She looked aristocratic and aloof, with dark rings around deep black eyes.

'Benedicte – Geordie; Geordie – Benedicte.'

'Enchanté.'

'Enchantée.'

The other had a prettier face but thicker thighs. She seemed fun, with an open, happy manner. Her name was Dominique.

Bobby announced, 'We're taking the Riva to San Remo and back. We'll be gone for a couple of hours. Wanna come?'

'Sure,' they replied in unison.

Carlo manoeuvred carefully out from the jetty, pointed the gurgling Riva towards Italy and opened the throttle. The full force of its 220 V8 engine pushed the bow skywards and they ploughed through the wake of lesser boats. It was not long before Monaco was a distant settlement on a crowded coastline. Carlo's face was immobile as he piloted the boat at 70 kph into the wind.

Benedicte leaned across to Geordie and put her hand on his arm. 'You look like the Little Prince.'

43

He arched an eyebrow involuntarily.

'Yes, you do. Have you read *Le Petit Prince* by St Exupéry?'

'No.'

'You look like him. Will you be my Little Prince?'

'Sure.' Without having a clue what she meant, Geordie agreed to be Benedicte's Little Prince. It seemed harmless enough. Benedicte smiled happily and kissed the side of his face. As their hair mingled wildly in the salty air Geordie looked in her eyes. She smiled seraphically and he felt oddly contented.

After racing to San Remo and back the Riva was met by Benedicte's mother on the jetty. She had a voice like flint on flint and was furious with her daughter, Bobby and Carlo. She turned to Geordie. 'And who is this?'

Geordie put out his hand and calmly introduced himself. 'My name is Geordie Kinloch; I'm at school with Bobby. How do you do?'

'Who is your father?'

'Oh, he's a diplomat – in the British Embassy in Paris.'

'You mean, he *works*?' she spat out contemptuously.

Bobby intervened, 'Hey, Geordie, let's split. We don't need to take this shit from her or anyone else. Let's go.'

As they left the jetty Benedicte pressed a piece of paper into Geordie's hand. Her mother grabbed her by the arm and the two boys walked briskly to the exit. The chauffeur was waiting.

'Back to the hotel, François.' Bobby turned to Geordie. 'That woman is the Comtesse de la Tourchette – she's utterly paranoid about men, where her daughter is concerned. Benedicte is probably the most sought-after girl in Europe. I saw you had a little secret with her. My advice is, keep off. She is *big* trouble: drugs, suicide attempts, shrinks – the whole thing.'

Geordie clutched Benedicte's note and simply responded with a thoughtful 'Mmm.'

Days passed, filled with unexcelled luxury, eating at Fanny's, dancing at the Maona, playing at the SBM Beach Club, racing the

Riva along the coast. Geordie managed to speak to Benedicte for long enough to get the address of her school near Lausanne before the phone was wrenched from her hand.

One night they staggered back to the hotel at 4 a.m. Bobby sat on the deep sofa in Geordie's room, rolling a joint. 'Hey, try this stuff. I got some new music in from Los Angeles today we gotta hear.' He took the cellophane off a long-player and slipped the disc onto the B&O turntable. They lay back taking deep inhalations of Afghan hemp. As he drifted away Geordie was treated to a new Californian band called The Doors. It felt like a wild animal was loose in his head... *'This is the end, my beautiful friend, the end...'*

It was late morning when he stirred, the curtains billowing across his bed. A breakfast trolley was wheeled into the sunny centre of the room. One side of Geordie's face was squashed flat against the pillow. His free eye could make out the faint wisp of steam curling from the spout of the silver coffee pot in the sunshine. He was living a Matisse still life. Bobby appeared. 'Hey man, it's 11 o'clock. When's your train for Paris?'

'Oh, late tonight; 11.55 or something.'

'Here's the deal. I get François to take us to Nice this afternoon. You show me the Platform; we leave you at the station. I have to be back here at 6.30. How does that sound?'

'Like a great deal; thanks, Bobby.'

Geordie was blasted out of bed by Country Joe and the Fish on the B&O system. His hangover from Afghanistan was more a disembodied carpet of flowers than a racking headache. He was spacey, cool, at ease and as ridiculously content as he had ever felt in his sixteen years. He savoured the coffee. He stared hard at the fluffed-up croissants. The pastry shone as golden as a wheat field, each flake as iridescent as a butterfly.

After a long shower he dressed in his Côte d'Azur rich boy clothes. He packed everything into the Louis Vuitton travel bag that Bobby gave him. He actually had little more than when he left London weeks

45

earlier, but everything was now upgraded and stylish. He had metamorphosed from a diffident, badly-dressed British schoolboy into a self-confident, tanned playboy. There were no limits to his world.

François drove the Bentley along the Corniche and up through the wooded suburbs of Nice to the Platform. The routine was still in place. Knots of hippies sat around making music with guitars and tambourines. Sleeping bags were laid out in a semblance of proprietary order. Geordie noticed how filthy everyone was. What seemed romantic weeks earlier was in fact out-and-out squalor. The hippies didn't even turn their heads at the arrival of another chauffeur-driven Bentley. They were used to being objects of curiosity from the cultured fringe of the Côte d'Azur.

Geordie got out and walked over to the far corner. He recognized the Mexican blankets, but not the blackened face of the wreck lying on them. 'Jeremy?'

'Yeah, what?'

'It's me. Geordie.'

'Great Lord in heaven, what happened to you?' Jeremy winced as he lifted his torso painfully off the concrete.

'I was thinking the same about you. Isn't it about time you returned to England and got your life back?' Geordie was shocked how Jeremy had deteriorated.

'Never going back. My life is here. Looks like you sold out, man.'

'I came to say goodbye, Jeremy. Take care of yourself.'

'Man, I broke the Rules. I deserve what I get.'

'Is there anyone you want me to give a message to?' The 22-year-old looked like an inmate of Buchenwald.

'Naa.'

'Au revoir. It was a great summer.'

'See ya around.' Jeremy slumped back painfully on his stained Mexican rug.

In the meantime Bobby had borrowed a guitar off one of the hippies and was thrashing out Bob Dylan songs. He had the same whining intonations as his idol and played better than anyone on the platform. He sat cross-legged on a rug playing to three girls dancing in a willowy abstracted dream. Geordie sat on the parapet overlooking the scented pine trees. Cicadas zizzed in the branches.

Geordie was left at the Gare Centrale later that afternoon. He positioned himself under the awning of a busy café and ordered a glass of chilled Kronenbourg. He stared with half-closed eyes at the bubbles rising through the amber liquid, tore a page out of his journal and began writing.

'*Chère Benedicte…*'

Remember Threekingham?

It was a glorious April morning with the sun streaming through the bedroom's south-facing bay window. He lay in bed watching her pad around the room, preparing her suitcase for the holidays. She had just showered and her blue silk dressing gown hung damply off her body.

'Right, that's it.' With a firm hand she slammed down the lid of her dinky red suitcase. 'That's all I'm taking. Time to get dressed now.' She slipped off the dressing gown and stood dithering, nude as a peach, for a few seconds by the wardrobe. She grabbed a pair of pink knickers from a drawer and eased them up with a satisfying snap as the elastic twanged against her flat stomach. She dragged a blue and white striped French sailor T-shirt over her head, then shook her wet blonde hair like a dog after a swim. A pair of white socks and finally she pulled on her tight jeans. The entire process took two minutes and fifteen seconds, he noted from the bedside clock.

'Pretty impressive, darling. And you look stunning. Some women take two hours to get ready and still look ghastly.'

'And who do *you* know who takes two hours, eh?' she laughed.

'It must be the bra that takes the extra time. You save a lot of time going without one.'

'I thought you liked it this way?' She pouted and pushed out her girlish chest.

'I think they're absolutely gorgeous – absolutely, unbelievably gorgeous.'

She jumped on top of him but he extricated himself quickly and shot out of bed.

'OK, I'm ready in eleven minutes.' She heard the flushing loo, the electric razor, the sputtering shower, the scrubbing teeth and the gargling, then he emerged from the bathroom in a flurry of Eau Sauvage aftershave and wet towels.

'You're as bedraggled as a bear in a ditch.'

'That's a good one.' He looked at the clock. 'OK, six minutes and we're gone.' White cotton shirt, a purple sweater, jeans, white socks and loafers. He tossed his washing kit into an overnight bag, threw in three pairs of socks, boxers, T-shirts, a pair of desert boots, a grey sweater, white slacks, his wallet, a camera, address book and his journal. Always the journal. He was 21 now and had kept a journal since he was 8. It was his lifeline to personal sanity. He was going to be a famous writer one day and the journal was his daily sketch pad. Just as Turner made sketches as he travelled around Europe, which were the precursors to great works, so Geordie Kinloch's Journals would be the precursor to the World's Greatest Novel. One day.

Evie had already positioned her case and handbag together by the door, ready to throw into the car. He took a last look around the room, tightened the taps, checked the lights, unplugged the electric gadgets, grabbed his jacket and stuffed the bags into the back of the grey mini van. He held the passenger door open for her and bowed '*Prego Signora*', then ran back to lock the flat.

As they drove away from the front door she cooed, 'It's exactly 8 o'clock, as planned. You're wonderful.'

'Absolutely not. It was all your planning. *You're* the wonderful one.'

'Actually… despite our precision start there is no plan for the day. This holiday we're on the gypsy trail. We'll just get in the caravan and go where the pony trots.'

'Don't you think it's romantic that somewhere Down South is a bed with crisp sheets destined to receive our warm bodies tonight? That bed could be anywhere within three hundred miles of here,' she mused, gazing out at the hills.

A thought furrowed her brow. 'Nobody knows where we are, not even my mother.'

'We would tell her if we knew where we were going. I would hate to tell her we were staying in the King's Head in Smithtown, only to end up in the Queen's Arms in Bogsville. She would be distraught if she called there and we hadn't checked in. It would spoil our holiday even if *we* knew where we were going, let alone your mother, don't you think?'

'S'pose so.' He didn't like Evie's tentative moods.

Within two hours they had passed Edinburgh and were well on their way south. The Border countryside looked magnificent in the hazy sunshine. Fluffy white lambs jumped and played in groups as cute and implausible as little stuffed toys. The winding road was lined with daffodils. Buds and catkins were in profusion along the river valleys. There was practically no traffic beside occasional tractors swinging on to the road carrying equipment between fields.

'You know, I'm never bored in your company;' she looked at him adoringly and laid her hand on his knee. He held her hand for a few seconds before putting it back on the steering wheel.

'I'm crazy about you, too.'

'Ever bored?'

'Never bored. I can always be myself with you.'

'We've known each other a month and I feel I've known you all my life.'

'Funny, that. You can really like a person and know them for years and try to make yourself love them but then you meet the real thing and Wham! It's all over. In seconds. Lightning strikes. Donner und Blitzen.'

'Do you think we've whammed?'

'We've whammed all right. If I died now I would feel fulfilled. I wake up in the morning at peace for the first time in my life. I was always impatient, intolerant, not very nice. Now...'

'You're impatient, intolerant, not very nice,' she teased, with a girlish laugh. 'Actually you're the sweetest man a girl could hope to mm...meet. I can't believe my luck.'

'Do you think we'll still like each other when we're older?' Geordie asked.

'I can see us passing our days together and suddenly we're 83 and wondering what happened to all the time.'

'Children?'

'Lots. Lots and lots and lots.'

'Dogs?'

'Lots of dogs. They would have to be dachshunds.'

'Staffordshire Bull Terriers. The finest breed in the world.'

'Yeugh! Far too ugly.'

'Dachshunds, then. But only smooth-haired chestnut coloured ones.'

'*No*, wire-haired.'

'All right, all right, wire-haired, but only one.'

'Four.'

'Four it is, then. As long as I get to choose the cats.'

'A big black fluffy cat called Elmer.'

'Elmer? *No.*' So the happy banter continued all along the switchback road into Northumberland.

As they drove into Corbridge, he pulled into the forecourt of the Percy Arms. 'Time to get out and stretch our legs. How about some lunch?'

They walked into the eighteenth century coaching inn and entered a low-ceilinged bar. Horse brasses, copper measuring jugs and hunting prints adorned the walls. A large stone fireplace held glowing oak logs and a Victorian grandfather clock ticked magisterially in the corner by the bar. The unventilated room smelled of stale beer and yesterday's cigarette smoke, an ambience not unfamiliar to them.

'I'll have whatever you have,' Evie went over to the juke-box and made her selection.

As the machine cranked up to play her song she said, 'Bet you don't know what I've chosen.'

'*American Pie?*'

'No.'

'*Imagine?*'

'Still no.'

'*Without you.*'

Just as his words came out the strains of Nilsson's love-song filled the pub. She kissed him hard on the mouth. 'Thank you.'

'What for?'

'For everything, for being you, for coming into my life.'

'I should be thanking you.'

The barman rolled his eyes at the banality of the couple's conversation. He had heard it all, many times over, from the village Lothario feeding lines to his latest victim on a Saturday night to the jealousies and arguments fuelled by whisky and Starbright Ale. Oh, the fights he had seen after a few pints of Starbright. That's why he kept the brass poker behind the bar. He remembered the time Horgan whipped it out of the fire and beaned Smithson for chatting up his girl. The police officer reprimanded him for keeping a potentially offensive weapon so close to the reach of unstable customers. He put it behind the bar from then on and used it for only two purposes – stoking the fire and threatening over-lubricated customers with brain damage if they didn't leave his pub immediately.

He had to admit that this pretty couple had an innocence about them. She was stunning, arty, leggy and spoke English too well to be British. He wasn't chatting her up or trying to impress her. They simply fitted like peas in a pod, a beautiful pair of human beings relaxed in each other's company.

'So, are you just passing through Corbridge?'

'We've come down from Scotland and have no particular itinerary. Can you suggest anything we can do around here for the rest of today?' Evie enquired.

'You should look at Hadrian's Wall and the Roman settlements around Corbridge. My favourite spot is Chesters, a few miles from here. The Romans really knew how to live. They had bathhouses, central heating, better houses than we have today. Mind you, they did have slaves to do the work, which is always handy. I wouldn't mind a few slaves myself.'

Evie put more money into the jukebox. *Without you* came over the air for the third time. 'Come on, let's go. We've got some exploring to do.'

Geordie paid and they left the pub. They visited the Roman settlement of Chesters.

'What amazes me is the permanence of these buildings. As that bloke in the pub said, the Romans lived well wherever they travelled. Every cohort carved its insignia in rock above the barrack gates. They took hot baths. You know, I excavated a an ancient granary near Hadrian's Wall a few years ago with a party of boys from school.'

Geordie became reflective for a moment. What he remembered most was the strong dislike the supervising master felt for him, not least because his wife showed up at the pub in Hexham each evening without him and was not averse to a roll in a tent with a senior boy afterwards. He had been one of the senior boys…

They scrambled down a slope towards the River Tyne and inspected the bathhouse. Hadrian's Wall was reduced here to a few blocks of masonry in sufficient quantities to know that some kind of wall had once been in place but it needed a rich imagination to fill the gaps. Nevertheless their imaginations played fast with the sheer scale of the Roman endeavours.

They ran excitedly around Housesteads Fort and marched for miles along the Wall until the evening haze signalled that they should find a roof for the night. It was a perfectly still evening and the slip of a new moon was rising in the Northern sky over the marshy moorland.

'It's such a shame we don't have a tent with us. I'd love to pitch it right here on the escarpment overlooking where the savage tribes used to roam and be spooked by Romans all night,' Evie announced confidently, knowing it was not even a possibility.

It was dusk by the time they returned to the car parked at

Housesteads. They drove for half an hour along back roads and eventually found a farmhouse offering bed and breakfast accommodation.

When they rang the doorbell the lady of the house answered and pointedly asked, 'You *are* married, I assume?'

'We're brother and sister.' Geordie looked across at Evie with a smile.

'Very well, then. Breakfast is from seven to eight-thirty. If you want an evening meal you'll need to drive to Twice Brewed, four miles up the road.' They were shown a small Spartan room with two single beds. The curtains were cheap and unlined. The 'en suite' part of the room consisted of a plastic screen around a poorly ventilated cupboard which contained a tiny shower and a toilet.

'This room looks fine. We'll take it for one night,' Geordie agreed, only because he knew there was no other choice within twenty miles.

'Here's the key. You can settle up in the morning.'

They moved their bags into the room and drove to Twice Brewed for dinner. The village consisted of little more than a stylish old-fashioned pub with a surprisingly comprehensive menu. They had a good bottle of South African chardonnay and enjoyed an excellent fish pie with fresh vegetables. They shared a sticky toffee pudding with vanilla ice cream.

'Mm… we've only been on holiday for one day and it feels like a week already. We seem to have done so much, don't you think?' Evie licked ice cream off her spoon.

'I was thinking the same thing. I loved our walk along Hadrian's Wall. You can really feel the Romans there. They still have a ghostly presence in this area. I don't know why everyone fought against them. They were so civilized and the benefits of law, roads and central heating are so obvious. Why would anybody fight it?' Geordie sat back in the leather pub chair with his feet pointing towards the open fire. He was feeling pretty mellow.

'Pride, probably. It's a man thing. I'm sure the girls were happy in the bathhouses with the Romans. The guys were running around with their bottoms painted blue and saw how superior the Romans were and felt stupid. So they fought to prove they were better.'

Geordie laughed at Evie's straightforward logic.

She continued, 'Like today's football hooligans. They're not much different from the barbarians the Romans fought. The forces of ignorance always resist law and order. It's all testosterone.'

The following morning at breakfast Evie told him how her Danish diplomat father died suddenly at their house in Corfu when she was 11 years old. Geordie talked about his divorced parents. Evie was the first to notice the disdain on the face of the farmer's wife as she served them breakfast. In mid-sentence she clapped her hand to her mouth.

'What's wrong, Evie?' Geordie was highly concerned. Perhaps she had bitten her tongue or scalded herself with hot coffee?

Their server returned to the kitchen and Evie whispered, 'We're supposed to be brother and sister. We told her last night.'

'Oh my gawd.' Geordie flushed with embarrassment and the rest of breakfast was muted and polite, as they affected to be familiar like siblings, not intimate as lovers.

They paid, packed the car and as soon as they were driving along the farm track to the main road, erupted with laughter.

'Oh, Geordie. My parents this, your parents that. How embarrassing!'

'You know, Evie, we'll never see that woman again. Never ever. She doesn't know who we are.'

'She might have taken your number plate.'

'And do what with it? It's not illegal for consenting adults to sleep in the same room. She won't come after us.'

'S'pose not.'

The next few days were spent in hilarious meanderings across the English landscape. They visited York and Beverley and found fossils in the rich mud around Scunthorpe. They drove along Ermine Street to Lincoln, staying in cute village pubs, exploring everything they could.

They had no time constraints, no agenda, no itinerary. If they saw a signpost to something that looked interesting, they turned off the road and investigated. They floated along in a cocoon of love, laughter and lightness and neither wanted to break the spell.

One particularly lovely morning they drifted into a village called Threekingham in Lincolnshire. It was a hazy fragrant English country spring day. Geordie stopped the car by the church of St Peter ad Vincula and they strolled around the daffodils inspecting tombstones in the soft sunshine. They pushed open the ancient iron-scrolled doors and entered the medieval building. The church seemed bigger to Geordie than such a small village could possibly support. The aisle was flanked with low gothic arches and the interior was flooded with sunshine, unlike many small country churches they had visited together.

'Black Death,' intoned Evie.

'What?'

'It says here that until the Black Death the Church of St Peter ad Vincula was an important parish church in a town of over a thousand people. After the Black Death the population never recovered, so that's why the church seems so big relative to the village today.'

'It's extraordinary to think that Threekingham was three times bigger in medieval times. But for all that, it seems like a much-loved church today. Look at this amazing flower arrangement.' Geordie sniffed a white lily in a vase by the altar.

Evie came over and smelled it too. They kissed. 'This is the sort of church I would like to get married in,' Evie squeezed his hand.

'Yes, these little country churches are so romantic.'

'I'm hungry. Let's check out a local hostelry for lunch.'

They found the Three Kings Inn and laughed as usual over lunch. Geordie read from a guide-book. 'Did you know there has been an inn on this site since AD871?'

'Everyone knows that.'

'Oh..... and that King John stayed here shortly before he died in

1216? That Henry VIII passed through here? And Dick Turpin's mother-in-law ran the place for a while?'

'What can I say, except that Evie and Geordie had lunch here on this lovely spring day? That's worthy of an entry in the guidebook, don't you think?'

'Definitely.'

After lunch they strolled around the village for a few minutes then clambered into the car. Evie kissed him and said, 'I'll remember Threekingham all my life.'

'So will I,' Geordie replied solemnly.

They drove silently for the next hour, their harmony punctuated only by observations on place names and the beauty of the immensely flat, fertile, wide expanse of the Lincolnshire Fens. Evie was map-reader and had a road atlas spread open on her lap.

'You know, Geordie, as we drive further south I am thinking that I should visit my mother in London.'

'We didn't plan to go to London.'

'We didn't plan to go anywhere. We're in a gypsy caravan, remember, going where the pony trots? It's just that we're now within striking distance of London and could pop by to say hello.'

'*Ubi tu... ego ibi,*' responded Geordie theatrically.

'That's very sweet, but you don't have to come with me. I'll take a train and you can stay with your aunt in Suffolk.'

'Let's go to London.' He turned the car sharply right, without warning, down the next road which vaguely, eventually, pointed towards the A1. With an irritated smirk he announced robotically, 'We're now on the way to London.'

'You didn't have to be so abrupt. Can you please listen to what I want to do?'

Geordie had not heard this tone from her before. He pulled over into a side-road and stopped the motor. Resisting the petulance rising in him, Geordie answered, 'Sorry. I didn't mean to be so sharp.'

'That's OK'. She looked him in the eye and said, 'Geordie, will you please respect what I want to do, whatever I say?'

'Whatever you say.'

'I want to see my mother and spend a night with her alone in London. I'll use the time to tell her about you, then you can come and meet her the next day. After that we can go on our way.'

'So when do you want to see her?'

'Tomorrow. I'll take a train and you can come down the day after tomorrow.' Noting the sulky expression growing on Geordie's face, she added, 'It's only twenty-four hours.'

Geordie mimicked, '*Only twenty-four hours,*' and restarted the engine. 'Well, we'd better find a place to stay so you can make your quick getaway in the morning.' He drove towards Peterborough.

Eventually she burst out laughing. 'It's like I told you I'm going to see another man. It's only my mum, Geordie – only my mum.'

He smiled apologetically. 'Actually I've been meaning to ask you about my rivals out there. Perhaps we should lay our cards on the table. Who fancies you and who do you fancy?'

'I will if you will.'

'OK – you go first.'

'Well, there's a guy called Etienne who says he's been in love with me for a long time.'

'I don't blame him. What's his story?'

'He's Indian.'

'Red or East?'

'East. From a rich trading family in the Seychelles.'

'Sounds exotic. Where? How? When?'

'At a party, through friends, two years ago.'

'Do you fancy him?'

'He's very different from you. Big, brown, flashy, insecure, Catholic. He's got something, but I don't think I could ever – you know…'

'What?'

'Go to bed with him.'

'OK, so he's not really a rival – just a suitor you're keeping at arm's length. Who do you fancy?'

'Well, there's Peter, my Literature lecturer. I quite fancy him. He's much older – 28 – he's engaged and the girls all think he's quite a dish.'

'Peter what?'

'Caldicott.'

'Why do you fancy him?'

'Well, he asked me out for dinner and was such a gentle man, yet quite forceful. He knows his mind. I find that very attractive. Now I've confessed my secrets, you can tell me about your other lovers.'

'There is no other love in my life.'

'You cheated.'

The day passed, the evening passed, the night passed. Geordie took her to Peterborough station in the morning. He was sad but respected her need to spend time with her mother. He decided to visit his elderly aunt in Suffolk to fill time on his way to London. Evie told him to be at her flat at 3 o'clock the following day. As her train drew out of the station at Peterborough he longed to be with her again. His pokey little grey mini van seemed hollow and irritating as he drove through the countryside without her, even when he played Booker T and the MGs at full blast.

It was 2.40 the next afternoon when he parked in front of Evie's flat in Onslow Gardens. Geordie didn't want to seem too eager, so paced around the block for twenty minutes before going into the building. He walked up the two flights to her apartment. On the door was a scruffy note sellotaped to the door.

> *Dearest Geordie,*
>
> > *Go to Derry and Tom's Roof Restaurant where I will be sitting and waiting for you.*
> >
> > > *Lots of Luv,*
> > >
> > > > *Evie.'*

The banality of the note irritated Geordie. The least he expected was to find her at the agreed place and time. He was not familiar with London so spent a long time finding Derry and Toms, then looking for the Roof Restaurant. By the time he found it, it was 4.15 and Evie was not there. No message at the reception desk. He was fuming as he made his way back to Onslow Gardens. As he arrived at her flat the door opened. A short fat Indian with a purple shirt and Afro hairstyle spilled on to the landing. He was encumbered with bags and suitcases. Evie was behind him, carrying a camera case and various shopping bags.

She gasped, 'Oh my God…It's Geordie. Er…I waited for you at Derry and Tom's and you didn't show up, er…so I came back here. Er…Geordie, this is Etienne Sobanda…Etienne, oh God…this is Geordie.' Evie was panicky at being caught *in flagrante*.

Etienne looked Geordie up and down as a dog might sniff another in the park. He exuded arrogance, gold chains and Brut. Geordie looked imploringly at Evie, as if beseeching her to prove to him that this wasn't really happening. In the middle of his turmoil, he was extremely British. He asked politely, 'How is your mother?'

Evie's eyes caught Etienne's. 'Oh, she called to say she was delayed in Amsterdam.'

Geordie stood staring at Evie without comment for a full minute and said quietly, 'So she wasn't here last night?' She didn't reply. She didn't need to. The full scale of Evie's treachery was already clear.

Etienne looked at his feet, paused a while and said, 'I gotta flight to catch so I'd betta be going.' He kissed Evie on the mouth. 'I'll call you tonight.' He nodded at Geordie, hauled the expensive baggage downstairs with a lot of banging and left the building with a slam. An aura of deodorant hung heavily over the staircase after he left.

'How could you, Evie?'

'It's not quite what you think.'

'How do you know what I think? What do you care what I think? Let me tell you what I think. I think you're a tart, a liar, a cheat and we have no basis for any further relationship. You have no conscience,

Evie. I can tell you're searching your addled mind for an excuse. Your only regret is that I found out. And for God's sake stop sulking. I'm the victim of your crime, not vice versa. I'm heading off now. Why don't you just call your lecturer and tell him all about it?'

He wanted to play the injured Hollywood hero and walk downstairs without looking back, but he wanted even more to see some sign of pain and loss in her – something to show that losing him meant something. He stood staring at her. She looked indignant more than sorrowful. The only satisfaction he got was her paralysis. She stood at the door with a long face, incapable of speaking. She looked in shock as he walked away. Geordie got into his now-hated car and headed north.

It was without question the worst, the saddest and the most dangerous drive he ever made. He prayed to die. He hoped that an articulated truck carrying steel coils would jackknife and slice the top off his car. He drew the line at suicide ('Won't give the bitch the satisfaction'), but if he was killed during this drive he reasoned that it would somehow be her fault and haunt her for the rest of her life.

The gods had other plans for Geordie. It was a long recovery, out of all proportion to the time he had known her, but the years passed and life mellowed. He found the excitement of new loves and financial success. For months, then years, then a decade, Evie stopped crossing his mind.

One November evening fifteen years later Geordie attended a function in a St James's club. The evening was dull, straight, self-satisfied and middle-aged. Quite awful, he thought, and started plotting his exit as soon as he walked in. He found himself cornered by a droning civil servant with halitosis, involved in some aspect of implementing building codes. A large woman of a certain age with bad skin and poor teeth came to the man's side.

'This is my wife Evie. I didn't catch your name.'

'Geordie – oh my God, it's Evie.'

The woman was astounded. 'Geordie Kinloch. It's you! I don't believe it.'

Other guests looked curious, hoping perhaps to see someone having an epileptic fugue. But they just saw an overexcited blousy woman having a fit, and went back to their conversations.

Geordie was repelled by who he saw. A huge weight dropped from his heart. He couldn't believe the years of sadness he had allowed himself to suffer as he grieved the loss of this frightful woman. He became jolly and laughed insincerely at everything she said. In the middle of countless 'whatever happened to a-b-c?' questions, Geordie elbowed her civil servant out of earshot and asked point blank, 'One thing I must ask you, Evie. Do you remember Threekingham?'

'Who was that? At Uni? Freaking who? No, I must have forgotten. Remind me about Freaking 'em. Was that a joke? Ha-ha-ha!'

By Jove, the Danish butcher's wife has come out in this woman. She's become utterly gross, thought Geordie. Aloud he said, 'It's no big deal. I have to go now, Evie. I can't tell you how much I've enjoyed meeting you again after all these years.' He kissed her porcine powdered cheek, noting the spider veins on her nose and the grey roots in her listless hair.

Geordie bade farewell to his hostess, left the club and skipped along Pall Mall in the damp evening air, just like Gene Kelly in the rain.

Santa Maria Novella

to Esther Read

As a young student Geordie Kinloch's feminine features conspired with a naturally soft aura to attract women and men alike. Even before he shed the chrysalis of puppy fat in his mid-teens he had learned to deal tactfully with suitors of all kinds.

He was also bright, personable and expensively educated. You might think these advantages would guarantee success on a grand scale, but here's the rub. He was brought up as a Presbyterian. From his earliest years Kinloch was imbued with the dusty mysteries of old ladies and the Scottish Faith. The word *No* was etched into his character and refusing pleasures was as instinctive to him as embracing them was natural to others.

His eyes were opened to the possibilities of the world when he travelled to France at the age of 16, but he was firmly shut back into his boarding school in the Highlands for nearly two more years. At the age of 18 he had a hilarious, if messy, encounter with a big, jolly girl in a wardrobe at a Christmas party. Then the dam broke. Opportunities for adventure were showered on him like ticker tape. In the euphoria, he was careless and didn't notice that he was making enemies. They were in two camps. Females who had been gently – always gently – dumped after sharing their charms. And jealous men. These enemies grew into a resentful mob which wished only bad things on him.

His nemesis arrived in the form of a female version of himself. She was stunning, blonde, bright, personable, attended a famous private school, German and a complete bitch. She had never met a male she couldn't control until Kinloch. Her motivation, if only she knew and if only he understood, was to eclipse other stars in her solar system. She didn't give a damn about his inner self, his aspirations or his fears. He was a challenge, plain and simple. Kinloch trusted the girl completely and simply couldn't see the bad in her that his friends warned about and his enemies knew only too well.

One evening he showed up unexpectedly at The Royal George to find her entangled in a discreet cubicle with her Russian lecturer. She had once talked of fancying the older man, but Kinloch ignored the cue. He noticed instantly their longing eye contact and the unmistakeable aura of new love. He was never one to make scenes, and despite her unconvincing efforts to explain, played the cool cowboy and simply left the bar without a word.

As he walked out he nearly suffocated in the North Sea wind. His heart exploded with grief. Rain lashed his face, disguising his tears from curious strangers on the street. 'How can this be happening? How could she? What a bloody fool I am.'

He paced the streets for much of the night until, exhausted, he slumped into bed shortly before dawn. He was sucked into a dead sleep which transported him for a few hours into a Caribbean dreamland of colours and laughter. When he awoke he was in good spirits for a split second, then it hit him like a steam hammer. She was gone.

He went to see his friend Scott, an earthy Virginian who was studying architecture. Kinloch pushed open the door of his flat, where he found Scott sitting at his desk. It was remarkably well-ordered, considering the rest of his room was a sea of filthy clothes, beer cans, brimming ashtrays, squint NFL football posters and half-eaten Chinese carry-outs. Boogie with the Canned Heat rocked from his stereo.

'Man, you look rough. Get stoned last night?'

'Scott, I need to talk. She dumped me.'

'Sorry to hear that, but why am I not surprised?'

'Don't go through all that "told you so" crap. I really don't want to hear it'.

'OK, chief, I promise; as long as you admit I was right – just once.'

Kinloch bowed his head and quietly admitted 'OK, so you were right. Just shut up about it from now on. Please.'

'I promise. Here – have a fag.'

'No thanks.'

Scott lit up and pulled in a huge lungful with his first drag. 'OK. You got three possible solutions: find a new girl, go away, or both. Sure, she's hard to replace, but there's plenty of ass out there.'

'But it's not *her* ass. I can't believe she's giving it to another man.'

'Fergeddit, Geordie. Move on. She was always using you. You're the only person at the university who didn't see it.'

'I can't jump into a new relationship so quickly. Besides there's nobody around I fancy.'

'Well, lah-di-dah. You really got yourself on a pedestal, sport. If you climbed down into the real world you'd find a lot of great chicks who would treat ya a hell of a lot better than your Princess Brat.'

'Nobody likes a depressed person. That's what.'

'Then you gotta go away. Travel refreshes the soul, cures a broken heart, blah-blah-blah. Find yourself a destination and prospect for new talent. When you've found some, let me know and I'll show ya what to do with it.'

Kinloch found his friend annoying sometimes, but a healthy counterpoint to his own introspections.

'I think I'll go to Florence,' he suggested.

'*Florence?* That's for old ladies and wusses.' He then mimicked a tour guide, 'On the right you'll see the Uffizi. To the left you can see the Uffizi. Straight ahead that's the Uffizi. If you could look through the roof of this bus, you'd see...'

'The Uffizi?' Kinloch ventured.

'No, dummy – blue sky.'

'So where would you go?'

'Where would I go? Fort Lauderdale, of course. It's Spring Break time. Best place in the world for unconditional pussy. Even you'd get it within twenty minutes of getting off the plane. There's a topless donut bar on the way from the airport. What more d'ya want?'

'What more indeed? I'll book my fare to Florence in the morning. Thanks Scott, great to see you.'

'Sure thing. Send me a postcard. Maybe they'll have a topless wuss joint there.'

During this exchange Scott didn't move from his desk. As Kinloch left the room he saw Scott swivel round in his chair, shake his head in disbelief and spit out the word 'Florence!'

Kinloch decided to take the train. He dreamed about the gradual unfolding of Europe from the maritime grey of the Channel ports to the emerald green of the French plains, yielding to sparkling Alpine peaks. Then waking up South of the Alps in the sunshine of Lugano to the scent of roasting coffee and warm bakeries on the platform.

From Ostend to Milan he shared a compartment with two lovely English sisters. They were on their way to see Venice 'before it sinks.' If he hadn't been so emotionally tangled he would have realized that that the older girl had more on her mind than watching Venice sink. She was fully prepared to push her younger sister into the corridor for an hour, pull down the compartment's blinds and offer him solace as they sped through the Savoy Alps. But he chose to miss the signs in his Presbyterian way and was mildly surprised that she forgot to give him their address when they left the train at Milan in the early morning. No doubt she found a latter day Casanova in Venice who... Idiot.

The train drew into Florence at noon and Kinloch ambled slowly through the streets towards the Mercato Centrale. He checked into his *pensione* in Via Nazionale and soaked for a long time in a bath. He lay on the bed and slept through the afternoon.

It was still and clear. All the bells in Florence tolled their deep, slow, solemn tones to summon the faithful to evening Mass. The bells reached into Kinloch's deep sleep and pulled him gently back into the world. He lay staring at the open window. A grey, sleek cat with green eyes jumped into the room from the balcony. He smiled.

'Well, old puss. Here I am in Florence. I have a week to explore and sort out my broken heart. What would you recommend?'

The cat wound itself around his hand as he dangled it off the edge of the bed.

'By the end of the week I will have seen the Duomo, Fiesole, the Bargello, the Boboli Gardens, Donatello, everything in the Uffizi...' He laughed, recalling Scott's disparaging comments about Florence. 'Yes, it would also be nice to meet new people from different parts of the world.'

The cat was on the bed now, quite at home with this stranger who spoke in a funny way.

'Well, a journey of a thousand miles starts with a single step. I'd better get up and start exploring this great city of yours.' He swung off the bed, splashed cold water on his face, dressed and slipped cash into the back pocket of his jeans. 'OK, see you later.'

The cat stayed on the bed and he left the room.

The evening air was warm and Kinloch slowed down to strolling pace as he left the *pensione*. He breathed in the shops, the churches, the people. The Florentines were fine-boned and stylish. Tourists stood out by their poor dress sense and bovine manners. Even he felt unusually crass compared to this beautiful race of Tuscans.

He was surprised by the free reign of cars, scooters and motorbikes. The narrow streets were abuzz with badly driven, farty little Fiats and tinny Vespas asserting their noisome right of passage. Glistening tour buses scraped along tightly like snow ploughs, forcing people into alleyways and shop entrances to get out of the way. Everyone seemed to accept that these hallowed streets should be commandeered by the internal combustion engine. Maybe Florence had the instinctive realization that cars would last only eighty, perhaps a hundred, more years. They were a passing inconvenience in the ancient life of the city.

He found a restaurant behind the Piazza San Spirito and was led to a table next to a group of American students. He wasn't really looking for company that evening, but was offered a glass of wine by one of the young women as soon as he sat down.

'Thank you – you're very kind.'

'Gad! Where's that accent from?'

'I'm British.'

'I am Emily, this is Joe. We're from B-U-double-F-A-L-O,' she sang in a good-natured voice, oiled by many carafes of Chianti. Kinloch loved the openness of Americans. They were uncomplicated, energetic and fun-loving.

'I'm Geordie Kinloch. How do you do?'

'Did you hear that? *How do you do?* Man, you a lord or something?'

'Just a common old bloke. Just Mister Kinloch.'

'*Just a common old bloke.* We're just common old blokes too, graduates in Fine Art from Buffalo University. We've been in Florence for a month on a study tour and we'd sure be happy if you'd like to join us, sir, for dinner. Our Last Supper in town.'

'It would be my honour.'

'*It would be my honour.* Man, you're something else.'

The evening sailed along with great mirth and conviviality. They consumed various dishes of pasta, veal and antipasto, drinking much Chianti and discussing all the 'must sees' for Kinloch over the next week. They finally tumbled into the street at one o'clock. They agreed to meet at his hotel at 8 the next morning. It had to be early because they were leaving by train early the next afternoon. He was promised an inside tour of some 'Perfect jewels that tourists don't get to see.'

Kinloch slept well and woke early, took a shower and sauntered into the hotel lobby at 8 o'clock. Emily was waiting.

'Hi, where are the others?'

'Couldn't get 'em outta bed.'

'You needn't have got up just for me. I would have understood.'

She took his arm. 'Come on Geordie, let's get breakfast. We've got places to see.'

As they walked Kinloch looked discreetly at Emily with sidelong glances. She was quite different from the jean and T-shirted student at the restaurant the previous night. She now wore a vivid green silk dress that sparked with the electric blue of her eyes. She seemed to be wearing nothing else and he could see no lingerie under the diaphanous silk. Her pretty feet were slippered casually in espadrilles. Her auburn hair was still damp from a hurried shower and she carried the delicious, light floral scent of Ralph Lauren.

They went to the trattoria across the road and sat down for a breakfast of cappuccinos and a basket of bakeries. Kinloch felt suddenly gauche and dry in the mouth. He was infuriatingly, embarrassingly tongue-tied by Emily's fragrance and beauty.

'We're gonna see Santa Maria Novella. Been there yet?' she asked.

'No,' was all he could say. He wiped the crumbs from an uncooperative pastry that seemed to have spread all over his hands and face.

'They do Mass at the Rucellai Chapel at this time. The rest of the church is empty of tourists and it's a great opportunity to look around without interruption.'

'That sounds good.' He could think of nothing more intelligent to say.

'Let's head over then. Ready?' She called the waiter, requested the bill in Italian and paid in one gesture before Kinloch knew what was going on.

'Please, let me pay for this.'

'My treat, Geordie. I've been in Florence for a month and I've gotta show that I learned some Italian. N'est-ce pas?'

They laughed and she took his arm again gently as they left the trattoria. He felt intoxicated by this creature, but puzzled. 'What about Joe?'

'What about him?'

'I got the sense that you were together.'

'He's an old friend, but not my boyfriend.'

'Just good friends then?'

'Just good friends. Why do you ask?'

'Curious. That's all.

Emily squeezed his arm softly and they walked the remaining distance to Santa Maria Novella in silence.

They entered the building and heard chanting from the far end of the transept. Otherwise the church was deserted, but for a priest hurrying to the service from the sacristy. Emily pointed to a huge painted crucifix hanging above the doorway. 'Attributed to Giotto,' she said reverently.

There were ornate fountains on either side of the door of the sacristy, one of which represented a simple landscape in painted terracotta. She whispered, 'Giovanni della Robbia,' then drew Kinloch to herself and kissed him on the mouth, adding, 'We have twenty minutes.'

They were young, they were beautiful, they were urgent. He gently leaned her against a baroque panelled cupboard and for twenty minutes of its ancient life the sacristy of Santa Maria Novella witnessed an ecstasy that excelled all the heavenly depictions of Bronzino, Vasari and Ghirlandaio combined.

Emily slipped the green dress back on as fast as it had slid off her body onto the marble floor. Geordie pulled up his jeans and just finished buckling his belt when the priest returned to the sacristy from Mass. He looked quizzically at the pair, who giggled like children. Emily took her new friend's arm again and they strolled slowly around the cloisters.

'So, Geordie, what did you think of that perfect jewel that tourists don't get to see?'

'Beyond description.'

They walked in contented silence for a while.

'Emily?' His head was awhirl.

'Yes?'

He turned and kissed her again.

'Emily, you absolutely *must* stay in Florence for the rest of this week. You can move into my *pensione* and we can explore other treasures together. Please, please.'

'Darlin', my train leaves this afternoon. It connects with a flight from Rome to New York tonight. My trip is over.'

'Then… why this?' He waved his arms ineffectually to indicate the scope of their new love.

'Because it was right.'

'Was?'

'Is, was – what's the difference? Geordie, I'd love to stay here with you but right now I have to get back to the real world.'

'What can possibly be more real than making love in the sacristy of Santa Maria Novella in Florence?'

'That's *really* unreal, Geordie. You know that,' she laughed.

He had never met a female who detached herself so comprehensively from *amore* so soon after the event. She was exactly like a man. Exactly like him. Only he was the one who wanted so much more this time.

'I'll leave you at your *pensione*, then I need to get back to mine, meet the others, change and check out.'

Kinloch meekly obeyed her orders and allowed himself to be deposited in the lobby of his hotel. She pecked him on the cheek. '*Arrivederci*, Geordie. See ya around.'

She turned briskly, left the hotel and merged into the throng of the streets. He was so stunned that he didn't notice which way she went. He ran to the street but it was too late. No address, no phone number, no surname even.

The grey cat lay on a pile of his clothes when he returned to his room. He picked her up, cradled her in his arms and slumped onto the bed. She started to purr.

'You're not going to believe this, pussycat….'

As the days passed Kinloch wasn't even sure if he had dreamed the whole thing; it had been as surreal as an encounter in a magazine.

He teamed up with various people over the week and steadily ticked off everything he wanted to see. He returned to Donatello's David four times. He loved to hover on the edge of tour groups and listen to what the guides had to say. He overheard one effete English academic telling his blue rinse audience, 'This is the one object in the Western world that absolutely *has* to survive a nuclear holocaust'.

Kinloch couldn't disagree.

On his last day the train was due to leave Florence at 1 o'clock in the afternoon for the return journey to Ostend. He was going to buy some tooled leather boxes for his family in the morning, but decided first to make a quick sentimental journey. He walked across to the trattoria where he and Emily had breakfast a century earlier. He sat at the same table and ate exactly the same breakfast. He imagined he caught a faint trace of her Ralph Lauren perfume.

He strolled the few hundred yards they had walked to Santa Maria Novella, crossing the road at exactly the same point.

Mass had begun in the Rucellai chapel. He stood in the empty sacristy and crossed himself with water from her fountain. He stood for five minutes on the sacred spot where they had communed, then followed their route towards the cloisters.

He ambled abstractedly past the entrance of a small vestibule off the cloisters. A brown-robed Dominican friar gestured energetically for him to enter, '*Vene, vene*'. The door was marked '*vietato l'ingresso*,' but he assumed the fat friar was authorized, so to speak, so he entered.

The friar closed the door and began showing him a smallish oval painting by Veronese. It was an allegory of the Republic of Venice. As he talked, the friar's fingers wandered towards Kinloch's thigh and upwards. Kinloch retreated as far as he could in the small room but his exit was blocked. The Dominican held his arm and eagerly showed more objects. There were two fifteenth-century globes, one of the solar system and one of the world. As he explained them his fingers continued their exploration. He had a smiling face and an oblivious expression in his eyes as he talked.

Kinloch's predicament was becoming critical and his brain worked furiously to extricate himself from the horny fat friar, when the door opened and a priest entered. The friar quickly looked innocent, the two clerics laughed and Kinloch bade them a most sincere *arrivederci*. He left the cloisters and raced back to his *pensione*.

Once again his grey cat companion waited on his bed and Kinloch scooped her up. 'Well, pussycat, if you didn't believe my last story, then take a load of this...'

A few days later Kinloch returned to university and went round to see Scott. He pushed open the door to the flat and tiptoed over familiar mounds of infested clothes and dirty dishes. Nothing had changed. Scott was at his desk in a cloud of blue smoke. He swivelled round and laughed, 'Well I'll be hogtied if it ain't Geordie.'

He paused, then, '*Well?*'

'Well what?'

'Well, how was Florence?'

'Oh, a lot of culture, a bit of adventure. It was a special experience.'

'More adventure than Fort Lauderdale?'

'No comparison.'

'I wanna hear all about it. Every juicy detail.'

'I had a kind of transformation in a church there. It changed my life. Things will never be the same again.'

'That's heavy, man.' Scott was mortified. Religion was outside his repertoire. He became unusually awkward and changed the subject.

'Princess Brat was here earlier, asking for you. I heard she was dumped by her Russian.'

Three weeks earlier Kinloch's heart would have leapt for joy. Now, his feelings for her were as flat as yesterday's beer. His experience with Emily and the Dominican friar had knocked the world off its axis. Princess Brat and her provincial conceits were banal and irrelevant compared to the forbidden fruits he had tasted.

'I've moved on, Scott. Everything changed in Santa Maria Novella. Everything.'

The Popsicle Man

to Marek Smrs,
a student killed working abroad on his summer vacation

The Greyhound stopped in the town square of Appendola, Ohio, at five o'clock in the afternoon. One passenger stepped off, the doors hissed shut and the bus roared off in a miasma of diesel fumes. Geordie Kinloch was left standing with a small suitcase outside the Appendola County Courthouse in a sweaty stew of ninety-degree heat and high humidity. He was vulnerable and exhausted but still had to generate one last volt of energy to reach safety.

He towed the wheeled suitcase across the road towards a group of youths hanging around a convertible car on the roadside and singled one out who wore a Green Bay Packers T-shirt.

'Excuse me, please could you tell me where Elm and Rockwell is?'

'Elm and Rockwell, man? That's combat zone. Why d'ya wanna go there, man? Where you from?'

'I'm British. I'd appreciate if you'd tell me where Elm and Rockwell is.'

'Fi' blocks down Maple over there' – he thumbed the direction – 'you get to Elm. Go right on Elm. Go through three long lights and you get to Rockwell.' He looked curiously at the newcomer in the town square wearing a rugby shirt, worn corduroys and desert boots. 'How you gonna get there, man?'

'I'm going to walk.'

'You'll get yourself killed way before you hit Rockwell man. Take a cab. Over there – Urbaszewski's Cabs.' They pointed at a green Cadillac parked in a bay outside the courthouse. 'Good luck, old chap,' one of them mimicked his accent.

Geordie smiled. 'Thanks.'

Conrad Urbaszewski was spread over the front two seats of the Cadillac, surrounded by empty fast food containers. He wore a sleeveless white nylon shirt with yellow stains at the armpits and brown stretch slacks to accommodate his bulk. His instant response when Geordie got into the back seat and said, 'Elm and Rockwell, please,' was 'What the hell ya wanna go there for?'

'I have a job there.' Kinloch talked to the beads of sweat on the fat bald head in front of him.

'Urban renewal?' A chuckle rolled through the blubber up Conrad's windpipe.

'Selling ice creams.'

'*Selling* ice creams? They *steal* 'em down there.' Conrad guffawed like a funny man at the circus.

'Please take me to Elm and Rockwell.'

Conrad shook his head and turned the car down Maple. Downtown Appendola consisted of the County Courthouse bristling with radio masts and reserved spots for six cop cars, a diner on the opposite side of the square, a line of old fashioned shops, a crude attempt at landscaping with cherry trees called Veterans' Park and a Carnegie Library. The urban sophistication of downtown Appendola rapidly gave way to streets of shacks, junked cars, scavenging pie dogs and burst fire-plugs where large numbers of laughing shiny black children splashed in the spray. A derelict steel mill fenced off by razor wire stretched along both sides of Elm for a mile, up to the first light. Central Ohio Hammer Forge flanked the next mile of Elm to the second light. A double track of the Baltimore & Ohio Railroad converged with Elm and Rockwell at the third light.

'Here's Elm and Rockwell, my friend. Which junkyard ya lookin' for?'

'Er, it's Pink Hippo Popsicles, 2670 South Elm at Rockwell.'

'2670 South Elm. Lemme see.' A crossing over the railroad led to a compound of low-rise industrial units. 'Must be over there.' The Cadillac bounced over the rails and turned into an avenue flanked by

75

more razor wire. They cruised along until they saw a padlocked gate in the wire. A painted sign inside the gate announced

PINK HIPPO POPSICLES
2670 South Elm.

As the Cadillac pulled up, two German Shepherds hurled themselves at the gate, snarling and gnashing, jumping and tearing at the wire.

'Those fellas mean business. Sure they expecting you here today?'

'That's what the letter says.'

'I can't just leave you here. Got a phone number?'

'It's on the letter.'

'We'll go to Kentucky Fry and you can call them from there. Ride's on me, brother.'

'I really appreciate your help.'

'No sweat.'

They returned twenty minutes later. The gates were open and the hell hounds chained. A tall bearded man in Hawaiian shirt, Bermuda shorts and steel-capped construction boots waited at the gate and welcomed Geordie with a knuckle-cracking handshake. 'Geordie Kinlak? I'm Jeff. Find us OK?'

'Yes, this cab driver helped me find you.'

'Yeah? Lemme show you where you' stayin'.'

Jeff led him briskly across a concrete forecourt through truck-sized plastic flaps into a glacially chilled packaging and loading plant. Six bustling women with quilted jackets, gloves and Elmer Fudd-style flapped hats were sorting piles of ice cream bars into boxes which were then wrapped in tight plastic and piled on pallets ready for despatch. Jeff waved his hand at the scene. 'Forty popsicles a box. Hundred boxes a load. Five loads an hour. Twenny-four seven from Memorial Day to Labor Day.'

Geordie's jetlagged brain soggily digested these numbers.

'Yes sir, four million popsicles last year. With yo' and

yo'compatriots' help we'll sell five million this year.' Geordie smiled sickly at these fantasy numbers.

Jeff shouldered a swing door into a tin-roofed extension with a concrete floor. 'We call this place The Shack.' The dormitory contained fifteen army surplus iron bedsteads with worn yellow foam rubber mattresses 'Take yo' pick. Five guys've already arrived so you can take any bed except where they staked a claim. Showers, basins and rest rooms are through there.' He pointed to a row of open showers and toilets without doors.

Geordie was glad to return to an approximation of room temperature. 'Thanks. I'll take this one.' He threw his case on a corner bed; at least the wall afforded slightly more privacy than the others.

'OK, you're free until seven tomorrow morning, when we induct the new drivers in the warehouse. Gotta get back to the plant now.' Jeff saluted and disappeared back through the swing door into the loading bay.

'Thanks. See you tomorrow.'

Geordie was shattered after the flight from London, followed by fourteen hours in Greyhound buses from New York to Appendola. He stripped off his filthy clothes and stood under a high-pressure shower for fifteen minutes, washing off the grime and sweat of his journey. He towelled off, slid into his sleeping bag and crashed out. It was seven o'clock.

He awoke amidst utter confusion exactly twelve hours later. The dormitory had filled overnight. The Shack was a cacophony of hacking, farting, laughing, flushing, unpacking, zipping, washing, brushing teeth and bustling for the big day. A small pimply English student with thin greasy fair hair bent down and looked Geordie in the eye.

'You'd better get up, mate; we're expected in the warehouse in a few minutes. We're going to be allocated our popsicle trucks and our routes. I wouldn't be late if I was you.' The Shack was already emptying.

Geordie shot out of bed, pulled on shorts, T-shirt and trainers, performed the briefest of ablutions, grabbed his wallet and was in the middle of the crowd of exuberant students as they rollicked excitedly towards the warehouse.

It was a building like an aircraft hangar, open at each end, containing rows of scruffy ice cream trucks. Jeff was standing on the tail of a truck, did a quick head count and started the session.

'Good morning, gentlemen. Welcome to The Pink Hippo Popsicle Company of Appendola Ohio. This morning you will be given your route and a popsicle truck. Your trucks have been loaded with merchandise and your inventory is listed on your drivers' seats. You all have three hundred dollars of merchandise at wholesale, worth four hundred retail. When you get back here at night please note everything you sold and hand the list and your takings to Mitch.' He pointed to a tall moustachioed man, who waved cheerily at the newcomers. 'The retail price of each item is advertised on the side of your truck. The money will be counted by machine and noted against your inventory list. After discrepancies are netted out you will be paid thirty-three per cent of gross sales every day. You'll then re-stock your freezers for the next day, which you'll pay for by that day's sales, and so on. By the end of your time with us you'll fill and empty your freezers many times over, but you'll leave them full, just as you found them.

'If everyone on your route is buying two-dollar Fudge Bombs then fill your freezer with Fudge Bombs. Don't waste freezer space with fifty-cent popsicles. You're here to make money. We're all here to make money.'

A cheer went up.

'Do your routes at least once a day. It takes a coupla days to know the best time to hit each street. Don't waste time hangin' around swimming pools at ten in the morning when you'll get great sales there at four in the afternoon. Go where there are lots of street kids. Position your trucks when church gets out. Catholics like popsicles after mass,

Lutherans at noon on Sundays, Missionary Baptists all day Sundays. Don't waste your time with Presbyterians – they don't eat popsicles. Over to you Mitch.'

Jeff stepped off the ledge and Mitch jumped up.

'Thanks, Jeff. You pay for your own gas. There's a Sohio gas station two blocks North on Rockwell where you can fill up each morning. Your trucks do twelve miles to the gallon, capacity twenty gallons. Don't run out of gas 'cos a popsicle truck stands out like a wounded deer in a forest of lions around here. If you have mechanical trouble, call the 800 number on the steering wheel. Keep to the speed limit, never argue with a cop. If you're held up, don't be a smart ass. Hand over the money. Theft ain't deductible. You pay for all losses, even if you have a gun to your head. That's the American way.'

'Blimey, how often does that happen?'

'Just be street smart, folks, just be street smart. Other questions?'

There was a reflective silence as the green English students digested the notion that they could be held up at gunpoint.

Mitch continued, 'No more questions? Your truck number is marked on your contract. Keys are in the locks. Your route is marked on a local street map with your contract. Every route should clear the salesman sixty bucks a day. Less than sixty you're not workin' hard enough. More than seventy, you got it cracked.'

Mitch called out names and handed out contracts and maps. Geordie's route was East Appendola. It started near the ice cream plant and sprawled over a huge area, part urban, part rural. He was lucky, as others had routes thirty, even fifty miles away in places like Elyria, Lorain, East Cleveland, Mansfield and Shaker Heights.

'Go for it, guys. Check your inventories, refuel and get on your routes. It's nearly eight now. Sell your first popsicle by ten. Be back here by seven in the evening or earlier if you sell out.'

Geordie got truck number 14, a chunky former US Mail Dodge. It had 428,675 miles on the clock. A sign on the dashboard warned *Danger, this vehicle is unsafe over 35 mph.* The frosted boxes in the freezer seethed with dry ice, not even hinting that they contained wonderful things like Fudge Bombs, Banana Bullets, Creamcicles, Neapolitan Sandwiches and Strawberry Shortcakes. He flicked on the chimes, as did most of the other students exploring their vehicles in the warehouse. The air filled with a horrendous mishmash of electronic childhood tunes designed to pull a kid instantaneously from the furthest recess of a property to the roadside, dollar in hand. Geordie's *Edelweiss* mixed with *She's Coming Round the Mountain, Good King Wenceslas, Danny Boy* and what sounded like the first bar of the *Marseillaise*. This impromptu concert drew a barrack square scream from Jeff: 'Shut the fuck up!' followed by the comparative silence of engines turning over in fifteen popsicle trucks. 'Now get on the goddam road and sell some popsicles.'

Geordie had never sold anything in his life. He was a law student and signed up for this jaunt at the beginning of the year after hearing a presentation at the British Universities North America Club. He heard a fellow student talking how he spent the summer selling ice cream in a Boston suburb. He made enough cash to buy a Chevy Camaro and drive ten thousand miles around North America. He sold the car at a profit and returned home with enough cash to buy a flat at University. Geordie joined BUNAC on the spot and got names of American firms which employed British students. He wrote to The Pink Hippo Popsicle Company.

He reached Munro Boulevard at the beginning of his route. Windowless one-storey factories and warehouses lined the road as far as he could see. The traffic was light and there were no pedestrians. He noted that North/South roads were mainly arterial boulevards named after US Presidents. East/West roads were shorter and numbered. He turned into 105th Street and stopped the truck beside a small white clapboard house. An old man was dozing in a rocking chair on the deck with a stick across his knees. A brown dog was chained to a banister rail next to him. Geordie turned on the chimes, *Edelweiss, Edelweiss, la-la-lalala-laa-la*. The dog went ballistic, flipped over, got caught in its chain and crashed into the rocking chair. The old man woke up, whipped the stick off his knee, pointed it at Geordie and fired two shots. One bullet cracked through the side of the truck, ricocheted through the freezer and exited through the wall six inches behind his ear; the other missed altogether. The old fellow grinned and brandished his rifle in triumph. Geordie put his hand up in a gesture of peace and shouted, 'Want a popsicle?' but the old chap started fumbling with his rifle bolt again. He drove on.

105th Street for the next six hundred yards consisted of similar properties. Run-down houses, worn out pickups, overgrown yards, old white folks. After two intersections he came to larger houses, equally run-down but swarming with young black people. He stopped the truck and turned on the chimes, *Edelweiss, Edelweiss, la-la-lalala-laa-la*. Scores of children, teenagers and young adults on both sides of the street stood and stared at the truck blaring out a tune. What was this white prankster doing in their neighbourhood? The youngest children had no fears. The truck was mobbed by small black kids. Soon mothers began to arrive to see what the fuss was all about.

'Watchoo doin' here, mister?'

'Selling popsicles.'

'Sellin' po'sicles? How much?'

'Prices are on the side of the truck.'

'I wanna po'sicle!'

'Me too!'

'Me too!' Mothers went back to fetch their purses and soon every child on the street was licking a Push-up, a Sno Cone, a Fudgcicle or a Bomb Pop. The women were curious to know Geordie's story.

'Where you from?'

'I'm from Scotland.'

'What's your name?'

'Geordie Kinloch.'

'I'm Irish. My name's Fitzgerald.' An enormous black woman convulsed with laughter.

'You married?'

'No.'

'How 'bout me?' She posed like a ballet dancer.

'Maybe, once I get to know you.'

'When you comin' back? We ain't seen no po'sicle truck here this year.'

'Tomorrow.'

Geordie repeated the performance every few hundred yards until he reached the end of 105th Street. He then turned left and left again and sold his last popsicle before he reached the end of 104th. He had just earned a hundred dollars in less than three hours. He returned to the Ice Cream factory for a refill.

Jeff and Mitch were sitting on the tailgate of a truck smoking cigarettes in the warehouse when Geordie rolled up. 'You're not s'posed to be back here till this evening.'

'I've sold out. I need a refill.'

'You're bullshittin' us.'

'Seriously. The freezer's empty and here's the cash.' Geordie waved a wad of notes and jingled an empty ice cream box full of change.

'You sold four hundred bucks of ice creams in three hours?'

'Yes. Now I need a fill up so I can cover the rest of the route. Adults like Large Hippo Sundae Cups, Neapolitan Sandwiches and Fudge Bombs; kids want Sno Cones, Push ups and Bomb Pops. Just give me six boxes of each. Should see me through till this evening.'

'Fill out the form and back your truck into the loading bay. I'll get the freezer filled right now.' Jeff changed instantly from bullying boss to the chief mechanic of a racing pit, performing a quick turnaround to keep the car in the race.

'By the way, I was shot at this morning. Old man shot a rifle bullet through the freezer.'

They examined the half-inch hole. 'Jeez. That woulda made a mess of your face. Guess he didn't like your popsicles. Watch yourself in those black areas, Geordie.'

'Actually it was a white guy. The blacks were very friendly.'

It was becoming clear that Pink Hippo popsicle trucks hadn't worked his route before. Every street was the same – a milling throng of kids clamouring for ice creams at every stop, day after day. Geordie became a local celebrity and mothers appreciated the entertainment value of a popsicle truck visiting their street. His daily earnings averaged a hundred and twenty dollars, a record for the Pink Hippo Popsicle Company.

He didn't have a clue about the territorial structure of life in the ghetto. He would drive from street to street, innocently crossing gang demarcation lines and back again. He often saw a crimson Cadillac cruising between 86th and 96th, but never outside those streets. It had whitewall tyres and wire wheels, white leather seats and immaculate chrome trim. *Mr Kool Breeze* was stencilled in gold across the driver's door. The driver was a great bull of a man weighing at least three hundred pounds. All gold teeth, gold chains and diamond rings. He wore white suits and frilled red shirts and never wore the same feathered hat twice. He would have done credit to Ladies' Day at Ascot. He cruised his territory all day checking out, and no doubt sampling, his financial interest in every brothel and crack house between 86th and 96th.

One morning a teenage boy hung back until all the other kids had been served. He did not ask for ice cream. 'Mr Kool Breeze says you gotta pay a hundred dollars a day to operate on his streets.'

'Oh really? I suppose he'll want a free popsicle next. Tell Mr Kool Breeze to take a hike.'

The teenage boy looked scared.

'Mister, you don' understand. I'm here to get a hundred bucks off you right now.' A long-bladed serrated flick knife materialized out of nowhere. He held it to Geordie's stomach. He froze. The knife was razor sharp and he realized he could be filleted in four strokes.

'All right, my friend. Take the money-box there. It's all I've got. It's got about thirty dollars in it.' The boy grabbed it and the bottom fell out, scattering quarters and dimes over a wide area. As the youth started to run away Geordie slid the door shut and locked it. He drove to a Gulf gas station on Jefferson and parked conspicuously on the forecourt. He stayed in the cab with his head on the steering wheel and couldn't stop shaking.

'You OK, brother?' A black attendant with Gulf overalls tapped on the window. Geordie unlocked the cab and slid the door open.

'Look like you saw a ghost, man.'

'I was just held up by a kid with a knife.'

'Where?'

'94th Street.'

'That's Kool Breeze territory. They'll take the shoes off yo' feet down there. It's no place for a white kid to sell po'sicles. It's no place for a *black* kid to sell po'sicles. Comin' to that, it's no place for *anyone* to sell *anything*. Lock yo' truck and come inside. Look like yo' needin' a break.' The man led Geordie into the building, behind the counter and into a back office. 'Hey Lucius, I gotta kid here got held up by Kool Breeze. Lucius, meet – what's yo' name – ?'

'Geordie Kinloch.'

'That's a fancy soundin' name. I'm Cicero Easton and this is my brother Lucius. Sit down. Here's a coffee.' Cicero poured coffee from a Cona jar into a styrofoam cup and handed it to Geordie. He sat down on a plastic chair.

'I really appreciate your kindness. Sorry I'm shaking. I'll be all right in a few minutes.'

'Yo' welcome, my friend. Take yo' time. Yo' in safe hands here. No point callin' the po-lice. They say you shouldn't never be there in the first place and stop wastin' their time. You one of them Swedish kids?'

'No, I'm from Scotland.'

'Two Swedish boys killed las' year in East Cleveland. Young boys just like you. Pulled outta they *Magic Ice* po'sicle trucks. Stab' an' beat to death. Them pimps don' like no po'sicle trucks cruisin' his neighbourhood. No sir. Nobody talk to yo' 'bout the ghetto?'

'No.'

84

'Seems that they ice cream companies hire foreign white students to sell po'sicles in parts of Ohio where angels fear to tread.'

'It's looking that way.'

'They watch and wait for yo' till it's safe to steal and kill. Never you go back to 86th and 96th. Where else you s'posed to be sellin'?'

'I'll get the map.'

Cicero studied the grid map of East Appendola and followed Geordie's route boundaries delineated in yellow marker ink. He whistled. 'Rough zone. But you could try the sou'-wes' corner, down here. White collar, church-goin' folks. Blacks and whites, good neighbours, swimmin' pools, kids in the park, barbecues.'

'I think I'll take the rest of today off. Go to the swimming pool and chill out.'

'Well, Geordie, if you ever need help, just holler for Lucius and Cicero Easton at the Gulf Station here on Jefferson. We'll be right out to help. Want some gas while yo' here?'

'Actually, yes. Fill it up. Thank you so much for your help.'

'Yessir. You always got a friend at Gulf.'

Geordie parked near the Sports Center. He lay out on the grass and wrote his journal in the sunshine between swimming laps in the Olympic pool. It was his first time off since he arrived in America two weeks earlier; he'd banked fifteen hundred dollars and had a few lively experiences under his belt. He wanted to team up with some of the lads from The Shack tonight, go out for a few beers – chill out. All he knew of America so far was loneliness, hard graft and street life at gutter level in one of the roughest neighbourhoods in the country. There had to be more to America than this.

Other students were evidently beginning to feel the same way. That evening Dave from Southampton University came back to The Shack with a used Lincoln Continental. It was an enormous shiny black charabanc, a cross between a hearse and a Mafia getaway car. Michigan plates, six years old, eighty thousand on the clock, twelve mpg – all for five hundred dollars including two months' all-risks insurance.

'Who wants a ride?' he enquired.

'I do.' Geordie leaped at the opportunity.

'All right, 'op in. We're goin' downtown to get somethin' to eat, then we'll cruise about the freeways to see what's what around 'ere.'

'Sounds brilliant.'

Four excited young Brits drove along with the windows down and FM radio playing Rock Classics. Warm summer air billowed through the car as Jerry Lee Lewis and Buddy Holly, Chuck Berry and Junior Walker blared into the night. They sat back in the deep seats and laughed a lot.

'Know what Oi think? Oi think Pink Hippo hires British students to sell ice cream around 'ere 'cos they know damn well that no American would dare to do it,' one of the lads opined.

'Funny how Pink Hippo has no American drivers, isn't it?' another added.

'They do actually, in nice places like Shaker Heights and Chagrin Falls.' Dave corrected him.

'Then they must 'ave their own depot. They don't mix with us plebs.'

'Yeah, we're like the Foreign Legion. They send us into tricky places and it doesn't matter if we get ambushed, 'cos we're foreign.'

They found a drive-thru Indiana Fried Chicken and bought two six packs of chilled beers at a nearby drugstore.

'All set folks? Let's rock n' roll.' Dave accelerated into the fast lane of the interstate highway and cranked the Lincoln up to seventy miles an hour. He flipped on the cruise control. 'Right, gimme my bag o' chicken and a beer. 'Ere's what Oi think. No risk, no reward. What summer job could you get in England that pays enough to buy a Lincoln Continental after two weeks? And when we finish we'll 'ave thousands of bucks to travel, buy things and 'ave fun. There's nowhere like America for opportunities like this. Oi'd far rather take my chances with a mugger on this job than sit in a noice office in Croydon, bored out of my skull doing work experience all summer.'

'Me too,' Geordie chimed in. 'I was mugged at knifepoint today. To be honest I was shit scared. The guy's eyes were as cold as a dead fish and my life meant absolutely nothing to him. But where else can you save fifteen hundred dollars in two weeks?'

Nobody gave a damn about Geordie's near-death experience. The beer and the thrill of tanking along in a Lincoln Continental on a hot summer night on the interstate overrode any desire to get heavy about anybody's experiences that day.

'Wot d'you get if you cross a Brit wiv an octopus?'

'Wot?'

'I dunno, but it can sure sell popsicles.'

'Yee-haa!'

A three-in-a-row no-break Rolling Stones feature started on the Rock Classics station. The first song was *Route 66*. Dave sang into his beer bottle, steering the car with one finger: *If you ever plan to motor West, take the highway, that's my way, that's the best....*Hey guys, there's a train. Let's race it. ....*Down to St Louis, cross the Missouri....*'

The interstate ran parallel to a service road flanked by the railroad. Dave swerved onto the service road at the first exit and drew even with the caboose of the freight train heading south. Geordie loved the romance of the old railroad company names on the freight cars. They steadily passed freight car after freight car, Chessie System, Union Pacific, Santa Fe All the Way, Chesapeake and Ohio, Erie Lackawanna...

'Wonder what they're carrying? ....*I hear the telephone that hasn't rung, I hear the knock on my door that hasn't come. You gotta tell me you're comin' back to me.* Illinois Central Piggyback, Norfolk and Southern, Union Pacific, Pittsburgh and Lake Erie, C&O for Progress...

They gradually reached the front of the mile-long train, hauled by four monstrous deep blue C&O diesel engines growling powerfully through the night.

'Let's race it to the next crossing.'

'Go for it Dave.'

'This is your James Dean moment.' Geordie egged him on.

Soon they were hundreds of yards ahead of the train but its relentless progress was marked by a headlight as brilliant as the beacon of a lighthouse. If the car slowed even fractionally, the light got closer.

'Up there – look, Dave – a crossing on the right.'

'Hang on to your beer bottles, folks.'

They call me the midnight rambler... Dave swung the Lincoln into a sharp right turn. Its broad stately tyres skidded as they crossed the polished rails, the car spun wildly and ended facing up the track towards the train.

'Holy Shit!' Dave threw his beer bottle out the window, flicked into reverse and wrestled the car backwards to the level crossing. The tyres smoked as they spun desperately for traction. The ponderous Lincoln jumped backwards over heavy wooden sleepers then leaped forward over the parallel track. It lurched down a shallow slope and came to a halt just as the train's klaxon screamed through the crossing. The freight cars thundered rhythmically past. Pacific Fruit Express, Norfolk & Western, Chessie System, Erie Lackawanna... finally the Union Pacific caboose with its winking red light signalled the end of their adventure and the train slid into the night.

The boys sat stunned in the Lincoln, shaken but unhurt. The car's exhaust system had been ripped out on the track and pulverized by the engines. There seemed to be no other structural damage. The chastened group of students limped back to The Shack an hour later, heralded by the infernal racket of a Lincoln Continental without a muffler.

Geordie stuck to most of his route but avoided Mr Kool Breeze's ten blocks. Most of his other streets were also in black areas, but there was no hostility as he made his rounds. Indeed, if he skipped a street he was missed by the kids and their mothers. But he was more cautious, locking the cab as he drove between stops.

Geordie had saved over three thousand dollars in five weeks. It was enough. He gave a week's notice to Pink Hippo and booked a flight from Cleveland to Mexico City. He wanted to explore Central America. The week went fast. He followed his usual selling routine, slackening off in the early afternoons to hang out with a crowd of American college kids at the swimming pool.

On the last morning of his job he was cheerful and exhilarated. A thunderstorm in the small hours had cleared the humidity and a light breeze filled his lungs with fresh air from the prairies, or so he fancied. Pale blue cornflowers nodded in the sunshine on the roadside and all was well with the world. He started his route on 105th as usual.

A small girl flagged down the truck, took off a fluorescent green stocking, fished into it for two grubby, worn nickels and gave them to Geordie. 'One root beer popsicle, man.' He didn't have the heart to tell the child it wasn't enough, so gave her the popsicle and a dime for change. She was thrilled, put the dime in her stocking and skipped off with the popsicle.

A muscular half-naked man stepped out of his home and waved down the truck. His equally scanty girlfriend waited in the porch.

'Watchoo want, baby?' he shouted back to her.

'I wanna banana split, honey.'

'I'll banana your split, baby.'

He then turned to Geordie. 'Gimme fudge, man. Two times.'

Geordie continued on his way, serving familiar groups of young children, their mothers keeping a watchful eye from verandas and decks.

By two o'clock the humidity and torpid heat had returned. He had sold out of most ice creams but instead of going to the pool to enjoy the rest of the afternoon he returned to the plant to refill his freezer. He decided to try the forbidden territory of Mr Kool Breeze one last time. He fetched his camera and drove to the Gulf Gas station on Jefferson.

'Hey, if it ain't Geordie!' Cicero Easton wiped his oily hands with a paper towel and clapped a muscled arm around Geordie's shoulder.

'Hey Lucius, look who's here!' His brother pushed out from under a jacked-up Chevrolet. 'Hey, man, we was wondering what happened to you. What's goin' on?'

'This is my last day selling popsicles. I'm going away tomorrow. I wanted to say goodbye and fill up with gas. I also need your address to send you a Christmas card.'

'Man, you don' hafta do that.'

'I really hope you make it to Europe one day. I'd love to show you guys around.'

'They have blacks in England?'

'Of course. Stand still, let me take your photo.' He snapped the grinning brothers at a gas pump.

'If we ever get away from this place we'll come visit. So where you goin' right now?'

'You don't want to hear this, but I'm taking a last look at 86th and 96th. I want to take photographs and sell a few popsicles if anyone wants one. If I don't get back here by 6 pm, come looking for me.'

'Man, that's not a smart thing to do. Kool Breeze is mad at yo'.'

'I'll take my chances. 6pm, remember?'

'6 pm. God bless yo'.'

The usual throng of children and mothers met him as soon as he turned on his chimes on 96th *Edelweiss, Edelweiss, la-la-lalala-laa-la*. How he hated that tune. It was his musical accompaniment to hell on earth, the seething American ghetto.

He photographed the kids as he wended his way selling ice creams through 96th, 95th, 94th and 93rd streets. It felt normal and he was selling as much as ever.

When he turned onto 92nd the familiar crimson Cadillac was parked sideways, blocking the street. Mr Kool Breeze sat looking straight ahead, immobile as a statue in profile. The only movement in the car came from the wind ruffling the long soft white feathers in his hat. Four athletic young men wearing identical back-to-front baseball caps stood motionless in front of the car, legs apart. They wore

90

wraparound shades and carried baseball bats. Nobody else was in the blocked street. A panicky dread surged into Geordie.

'What would my father do in this situation? He wouldn't have been so bloody stupid as to be here in the first place. Well, there's no defence like offence. Go down fighting. It's your only chance matey. *Fortuna favet fortes.* Yee-haa!' He was inflamed with a heady mix of British public school spirit and Confederate bravado. He slid up the windows, checked the locks and accelerated towards the group of choreographed gangsters. He gambled that Kool Breeze valued his Cadillac more than he valued the old Dodge truck and would shift his ass when he realized that this mad Brit meant business. The truck built up to full steam and barrelled towards the roadblock. Geordie aimed for the tight gap between the back of the Cadillac and a fire-plug on the sidewalk.

'If you've got to take a narrow gap, take it fast.' Geordie repeated the old racing mantra, his foot almost through the floor. His Immobile Koolness freaked out, turning his precious Cadillac sharply at the last moment to avoid a collision. The Kool youths scattered. Geordie clipped the fire-plug on his way through and a high-pressure geyser erupted over the scene, drenching Mr Kool Breeze and his immaculate white upholstery, as well as his four henchmen.

'So far so good. Four more streets and I'm out of his territory.' He turned left down Madison, passed 93rd and 94th. There was a red traffic light at Madison and 95th. Normally in the circumstances he would have cracked through the red light, preferring to argue the toss with a cop than with the Kool Breeze Summary Justice Department. But the intersection was busy and fast. He stopped. Within seconds there was a thump at the back of the truck. He saw in the mirror that two youths were clambering on the metal step and trying to smash open the rear doors. The lights turned and he accelerated up to full speed. The youths hung on like Keystone Cops. Geordie then rammed the brakes hard. There was a simultaneous double bang as two heads cracked into the back of the truck. He accelerated away again, leaving two dazed thugs sprawled on the busy concrete highway behind him. At 5.45 he checked back at the Gulf Station.

'Glad to see yo' back, Geordie. Goin' home now?'

'Yes. Thanks for everything. Keep in touch.'

A massive thunderstorm broke. Sheets of torrential summer rain cascaded over Appendola County. Geordie drove slowly back to the Pink Hippo depot.

By 6.30 the clouds had cleared, leaving a red streak across the western sky. Steam was rising from the earth, sifting upwards through the grass and the trees and the telegraph poles and all the houses and outhouses. The sun was an enormous glow on the horizon and there was not a breath of wind.

Geordie parked his old Dodge in the warehouse for the last time. Jeff took a cursory look around the vehicle for damage, signed a release form, tore off a duplicate and passed it over.

'My man, you did real good this summer. Give us a call if you ever wanna come back. You always gotta place at Pink Hippo.' He administered a bone-cracking handshake.

'Thanks, Jeff. I appreciated the chance to work here.' Geordie folded the paper and put it in his pocket. He turned away and couldn't help grinning. Jeff hadn't noticed two perfectly symmetrical dents in the rear doors of his truck.

The Revolution

to Roddy Martine

'In 1975 Britain was on the brink of civil war. I know, because I intended to start it'. Kinloch drew on his pint and put the glass down carefully on the stained beer mat. His words were not in the bragging tone of a habitual drunk, but quietly spoken and authoritative. He stood with his back to the bar, talking with his friend Steve, a local building contractor.

'Looks like we've got a lively evening ahead.' The barman smiled. He had known Kinloch for years, but was always curious to fill the many gaps in his knowledge of the man.

'The country was suffering under one of Labour's chronic flirtations with Marxism, with its dismal record of punitive taxation and low expectations. The trade unions forced an election which destroyed the Conservative government in 1974 and were rewarded with heavy pay increases by Labour's stooges. The coal-miners got a 29% pay increase, paid out of my taxes. I loathed the greyness of enforced equality that seeped out of Labour like pus from a corpse. They called it Social Justice.'

'It's getting like that today under these jokers in Westminster. I'm just an ordinary working bloke. Absolutely sick of all these stealf taxes and regulations.' Steve was already getting worked up.

'I can't comment on today, but in 1975 Labour and the unions had Britain by the balls. For me the last straw was just after the railwaymen were awarded a huge pay rise. I was meeting someone off a train at Waverley Station and asked a fat ticket collector sitting on a stool whether the train was on time. He said, "Ask at the Enquiry Desk." I replied, "Why can't you tell me?" He got shirty and said, "It's my job to inspect tickets, not answer enquiries." I replied, "You've just got a 30% pay rise at public expense. Why don't you get off your fat arse and provide a service?" He was stunned. Nobody spoke to a union brother that way. I turned to walk away and he yelled until I was out of earshot. That evening I went to the Drill Hall at East Claremont Street and joined the Territorial Army.'

'You joined the army because you had a spat with a ticket collector?' Steve laughed.

'I joined the army because I wanted to learn how to shoot straight when the revolution came. I was sick of the country being in the hands of such scum.'

'Cor. Go on, then.' Steve rubbed his hands with relish.

'I joined the Royal Scots Company of the 2/52 Lowland Volunteers in Edinburgh as a private soldier. The funny thing was that other young university fellows were there with similar ideas. We had no problem getting into the Officer Cadet stream.'

'Why didn't they spot you as troublemakers?'

'I didn't exactly go to the recruiting officer and say, "I want to start a revolution, teach me how to shoot". It was more subtle. I wanted to train as a professional soldier, quietly plan a coup, choose my moment, rise up and destroy the Left in a surgical civil war.'

'Wee fascist bastard.' By this time other men had joined Kinloch's little audience at the bar. One drove a delivery truck for the local brewery. His reddish hair was cropped tightly and a ring hung from his right ear. His wiry arms were tattooed with satanic imagery and, bizarrely, a red love heart with 'Mum' inscribed in its centre. The only reason Kinloch was not thrashed to a pulp in this drinking house was that his tone was at odds with the inflammatory views he expressed. He sounded like a world-weary BBC reporter, not a right-wing toff. Besides, they were all curious to hear where the story was going.

'Fokk, so they let you in just like that?'

'Just like that. The problem was that British Army training at the time was focused on fighting Russians on the plains of Eastern

Europe. Army doctrine was to channel the Russian army into killing zones and destroy them, with tactical nuclear weapons if necessary. It was entertaining to learn how to melt Russians in their tanks, but it didn't train me for the kind of war I wanted to start. I needed to learn about hearts and minds, insurgency – Ho Chi Minh rather than Rommel.'

'Aye, Ho Chi Minh was a guid lad. Kicked French arses in Vietnam.' Tattoo showed a surprising grasp of history.

'Whatever. My first Saturday out with the Territorials, I reported to the Drill Hall at six in the morning. We were shown how to pull apart and reconstruct a standard army rifle, sub-machineguns, light machineguns and the GPMG – General Purpose Machinegun. We then piled into the back of a four-ton truck and were driven to the shooting range.

'The army shooting range at Dreghorn was exposed and it was bitterly cold. While the Jocks stamped about trying to get warm I volunteered for everything. I started in the butts under the targets, flagging the shots. Bullets cracked into the wooden targets only three feet above my head and thudded into the frosty bank beyond. I remember the little kick of earth as the bullets hit, sometimes accompanied by a wisp of smoke in the seething ground. When it was my turn to shoot, the sun was in my eyes and I remember the arc of heavy machinegun bullets glinting in the sunlight as they curved over and smashed into the target. Such power and beauty. I thought of Downing Street.'

'I'd ha' thought o' that parliament-load o' pricks in Holyrood. Useless parasites. They couldnae organize a pissup in a brewery.' Tattoo grinned.

'Aye, I'd love to mow doon that crowd o' self-important dick-heids'. His friend laughed, revealing a mouth of dirty, broken teeth.

Kinloch waited for his audience to finish their contributions and continued. 'In the truck on the way home my sergeant said he was pleased with my progress. We got talking. His name was McTaggart and he was a decorated veteran of the Korean War. He worked in a coal-mine south of Edinburgh. He told me that most of the men in the platoon were miners from the same pit.'

'So you planned to destroy the unions and most of your fellow-soldiers were coal-miners?' Steve didn't miss a trick.

'Quite so.'

'Ye really screwed up there, pal.' Broken Teeth wiped beer froth from his face and guffawed.

'I asked Sergeant McTaggart if I could visit his coal-mine. He said they rarely allowed outsiders down the pit, but as a shift foreman he could arrange unofficially for me to come down with him one day the following week. He gave clear instructions, "You've got to sound Scottish, like me, surr, or they'll smell a rat. If they ask, say you're a journalist from the *Daily Worker* writing aboot the brave boys doon the pits."

'I practised my glottal stops and grunts for the next few days and presented myself at Gilston Glen Colliery at 5a.m. the following Thursday.'

'You patronizing wee shite.' Praise indeed from the Tattoo. All that seemed to prevent Tattoo and Broken Teeth from smashing their glasses into Kinloch's face was their curiosity about where the story was going.

'Maybe – but it got me down a coal-mine.' He continued, 'McTaggart met me in the car park and repeated that I must say as little as possible. I was lent a yellow hard hat, emergency breathing apparatus and overalls. As the group of twelve of us filed into the cage, we were handed leaflets by a thin man with glaring black fanatical eyes. McTaggart whispered, "You've got to get past the Commissar. Take a leaflet, look at the ground and don't say a word." I did as I was told, we were locked into the cage and dropped, freefall like a boulder, for 2,500 feet. In the dim light I read my leaflet. It was urging miners to class solidarity against the filthy capitalists. They wanted to build a fighting fund for another strike, another 30% pay rise. There was also an advertisement for subsidised holidays to the Crimea. Subsidised by whom, I wondered? Finally the cables took the tension and the cage slowed to a stop.

'A group of tired, grimy miners stood waiting at the bottom after the midnight shift. They filed into the cage without a word as we filed out without a word. We walked along a well-lit, low tunnel to a miniature roofless train.'

'So you mean to say that you were stuck down a coal-mine with a group of communist coal miners? What on earth were you thinking? These were the guys you joined the Army to fight.' Steve's mouth was agape.

'I saw it as an exercise in knowing my enemy. I was spying on their world. As we sat on metal benches on the train, McTaggart nodded towards the leaflet in my hand, saying, "We're no' Commies. It's those middle-class educated bastards who cause all the trouble. That shite at the top of the lift has never worked a day in his life. But he can get the Union to call a strike at a moment's notice. If he doesn't like the look o' ye he'll pull ye off shift and ye lose a day's pay. He's in touch with every commissar in Scotland and calls a wildcat if he feels like it."

'McTaggart had fought Communists in Korea and was a solid, honest working man with no agenda. He didn't fit the fanatical coal miner image of the popular press. The others on the shift also seemed like competent, hard-working, decent men. I had heard how the KGB infiltrated the British Labour movement, and it began to make sense.

'The train took us horizontally two miles further into the bowels of the earth. It stopped at the head of an access tunnel leading to the coal-face. It was only four feet high so we stooped and scrambled along for hundreds of yards. It was silent but for the creaking and groaning of pit props and the dripping of water. Naked bulbs hung every twenty feet or so, attached to improvised wiring.

'At the end of the tunnel was a chamber where a giant slicing machine with circular blades moved back and forth across the coal-face. It cut the coal in slabs that fell on to a conveyor belt. Great hydraulic rams kept the steel cutter hard against the coal seam, which ensured uniform slices every time the blades swept across. Powerful lights played into the scene through thick dust. Every man had an exact job and stood by the machinery like an artilleryman by his gun. It was an infernal scene but I was astounded by the hard efficiency and teamwork of the miners.

'McTaggart signalled our arrival to the outgoing foreman and we took over the shift without breaking step. Our men took their positions and the machine kept slicing. I was given a spade and ordered to shovel fallen coal back on to the conveyor.

'About three hours into the shift the machine was stopped. It had hit a pocket of sandstone and needed to be realigned. As the men retracted the hydraulic rams the machine came away from the wall. A huge piece of rock fell in from the roof followed by a surge of water. At first I assumed this was a normal event. You go down a mine for the first time, the roof collapses and the tunnel fills with water. It must be normal.'

Kinloch stopped and looked around. His audience was no longer cocky. They stood around in a semicircle with pints at their chests, expectation on their faces like a group of children at story time.

'You'd never find me down a coal-mine, never ever. What happened when the roof fell in?' Broken Teeth urged him on.

'Well, McTaggart ran for the emergency phone. He was calm but urgent, telling them to be prepared to close the anti-blast doors and contain the flood. He then shouted at me, "Surr, run back up the access tunnel as far and as fast as ye can. There's nothing ye can do to help here."

'I hesitated. Freezing black water was steadily filling the tunnel and I shouted back, "I don't think there's a hell of lot you can do here either. You have to come too."

'"Surr, it's my job to contain the water and save the machinery." He then added, "Miners and soldiers die every day. I've seen worse. Now go!"

'The other men stuck to their posts like Royal Navy stokers in the engine-room of a sinking battleship. They said nothing. I felt a complete coward as I ran feverishly up the tunnel. Water was up to my waist by the time I reached the junction. Further back I could see that it was almost up to the roof and most of the lights were submerged. I ran as fast as I could up the incline of the railway tunnel. After about two hundred yards it was dry and I sat on the steel rails to catch my breath. A klaxon rang behind me and orange lights flashed. Two huge steel hydraulic doors closed silently, sealing off the working tunnels from the rest of the mine.'

There was complete silence in the pub as each listener digested the horror of Kinloch's predicament. What would they have done? He was describing a situation close to many peoples' worst nightmares.

'Three minutes slower and I would have been sealed on the wrong side of that door. Nothing could survive behind there. I had left McTaggart and the others to die. There was nothing I could do to help, but I was utterly ashamed of myself. I was soaked, freezing and frightened as I trudged along the railway. I knew it was about two miles before I reached the bottom of the main shaft and wondered how I would explain myself to the rescuers, let alone that sneering Commissar. My visit to the mine was highly unofficial and they might associate my sole survival with bad karma or even sabotage.'

'Aye, ye wuid be a prime suspect after they found out what ye thought aboot the miners.' Tattoo liked the irony of Kinloch's position.

'Absolutely.' Kinloch sipped his beer and resumed, 'There would have been enquiries, I would have been cross-examined as a suspect, my story picked over again and again. I've no doubt that I'd have been exonerated, but the smell of cowardice would have hung over me for the rest of my life.

'I passed many tunnels leading to old workings on both sides of the track. The silence was crushing but they seemed haunted with the dramas they had witnessed over the past hundred years, the men, the ponies, the boys, the tragedies, the near-escapes. Now they were black voids barred by iron gates, collapsing in on themselves as the pit props finally snapped or contorted out of all usefulness.

'From a side gallery I saw lights moving and heard a metallic clanking. A train! I stepped off the tracks and waited. The train stopped when the driver saw me and I immediately heard a familiar voice from the carriage behind, "Thank God you're all right. We wondered if you'd got through the sealed gate in time." McTaggart jumped off the train and shook my hand. He was drenched and bedraggled but a broad grin shone through his coal-blackened face. The other shift workers leaned out of the carriage, looking like a grinning cast of Black and White Minstrels. None was missing and they were all thoroughly soaked. I asked McTaggart how he had escaped.

'"We nicked through the conveyor tunnel before the workings flooded completely. Had to swim underwater for a few yards. I lost the machine but they'll pump it oot."

'I told him how I had got through the gate with just a few minutes to spare. Nobody said anything as we jolted along the underground railway line to the lift. I just sat with a sense of relief for our incredible good fortune.

'Later, in the showers, I heard McTaggart talking with his friends about a pigeon race he was organizing. Others talked about the recent victory of Hearts over Celtic. Nobody mentioned the incident in the pit. As I left the colliery I thanked McTaggart and said that he should get a medal for saving the lives of his team. He looked puzzled.

'"Oh that? That's all in a day's work, surr. I've been in a worse fix before and I've nae doot I'll be in a worse fix again. See ye on Saturday at the Drill Hall to practise the parade for Remembrance Sunday." McTaggart looked wistful, adding, "Aye. Now *those* were the brave men, surr, the very cream of the crop." He turned towards his rusty old Ford in the car park and gave me a brief wave.

'That night I decided to postpone the civil war. I had some

rethinking to do. It was going to be more complicated to confront and destroy the enemy than I originally thought. The enemy was a handful of trained agents infiltrating British life with Russian backing. Cheap holidays in the Crimea, my arse. The British army doctrine of channelling the Russian army into killing zones was probably right after all. To get rid of the KGB agents in Britain, you needed to kill the queen wasp and destroy the nest.'

The pub had gone through its full evening cycle and it was now time to close. The motley knot of drinkers around Kinloch had dispersed and the Tattoo said he would walk part of the way back with him. As they finally parted outside the diner where the Tattoo habitually ate, he hugged Kinloch drunkenly and promised, 'If you ever wan' a pal to carry yer machinegun, ye know where tae find me, surr.'

'I'll bear it in mind. Goodnight.'

The Contrarian

to my father

Aristide Chatel was Belgian, meticulous in dress and formal in manner. There were no nuances when he spoke to people from different backgrounds; he squared up to everybody and was a gentle and honourable man. He was one of a handful of characters Geordie Kinloch recalled fondly from his early days at the bank. Unlike other directors he gave time generously to the younger staff. He was never dismissive and when it became obvious that someone hadn't understood what he was talking about, he would repeat everything he had just said, more simply and in a kindly manner.

He was famous among his youthful followers at the bank as a stock market player. Kinloch enjoyed it when he held forth across the trading floor to nobody in particular. Whenever he began one of his homilies there would be a groan from the Cockney dealers – 'Oi, Belgie, belt up!'

Out of the blue he would come out with homespun truisms: 'You know, it takes true perversity to sell into a stock market uptrend. When everyone is bragging about the money they are making in the market, why do I sell everything and watch those stocks continue to rise without me? I've got into a lifeboat expecting the ship to sink, but all I hear is the sound of laughter and clinking glasses gradually fading as the cruise liner steams off into the sunset without me. It's the same when I buy in a falling market. When shares look cheap I dive on them like a hawk. But the market sometimes keeps falling and the price I pay looks more stupid as each hour passes.'

Chatel was a mine of Wall Street jokes circulating at the time of the 1929 Crash. 'Hear this one. A young man sat crying on the steps of the New York Stock Exchange. A stockbroker asked him what his problem was and he replied, "I've got Syphilis at 28."

"'That's nothing buddy, I got Chrysler at 84.'"

Despite his self-deprecating admission of losses and forgone opportunities Chatel was in fact a formidably successful investor. Well into his sixties, he was at his intellectual prime and not apparently threatened by the youthful world of investment management. His method was to establish the group consensus then take exactly the opposite position.

He was an Honorary Professor of Finance at the local university business school, where he lectured to graduate trainees – 'financial cannon fodder', as he described them. His lectures were popular because they combined technical knowledge of investment markets with juicy anecdotes from the financial trenches. He always wore a bow tie in the manner of American wannabe attorneys and dressed impeccably for his lectures. Kinloch went to one lecture before leaving the bank to see what they were all about.

At one point, Chatel tapped the side of his nose and his class looked expectant. 'If I teach you one thing on this course, it is to learn how to smell. The smell of *consensus* pervaded the stock market in 1999.' He spat out the word like a piece of bad fruit.

'Let me give you an anecdote. A financial planning firm in Los Angeles gave a Five Billion Dollar Party for its clients and staff in January 2000. Every client portfolio had risen substantially in 1999 and money was pouring through the door like a water-jet from a fire hose. As the Moët fizzed in their glasses the chief executive addressed the happy throng. He congratulated his staff for their astuteness in investing 80% of every client portfolio in technology stocks. That decision alone increased the sums they controlled from $3 billion to over $5 billion in one year.

'One guest at the party questioned the consensus. He dared to suggest that they should sell technology stocks after their huge move and invest the proceeds in a depressed sector. Energy perhaps, or a bond fund. Even stay in cash until better values opened up in the market. His suggestion had the effect of a character in a Bateman cartoon, "The Bounder who pissed in the punchbowl at the Five Billion Dollar Party".'

The students in his lecture chuckled.

'Our hero was ridiculed, but the following day he sold every American stock he owned. He sidestepped the ensuing stock market collapse and stayed in cash for the next twenty months. Only then, when fear was rampant, did he venture back into the stock market. He mainly bought technology stocks, for a small fraction of their price at the time of the Five Billion Dollar Party.

'Ladies and Gentlemen, I was that guest. I'm not telling you this story to show that I'm a genius, because I'm not. I just follow one simple rule to make and preserve money in the stock market. That rule is, always take the opposite view when the consensus is in one direction. It never fails. Some people call it perversity – others call it moral courage; I call it common sense.'

Fuelled by his stories Kinloch graduated from the City. He lost touch with many of his former colleagues, occasionally wondering what had happened to his Belgian mentor. He hoped that one day younger people might think of him in the same light as he regarded Chatel.

One autumn afternoon a few years later Geordie was walking through Green Park towards Pall Mall when he saw a familiar anachronistic figure sauntering towards him. The figure wore a bowler hat, a trimly-tailored navy cashmere coat and a furled umbrella in the manner of City gentlemen before The Beatles. He was the very model of a 1950s London businessman – only he was Belgian and it was the twenty-first century.

'Monsieur Chatel?'

'*Oui?*' He looked quizzically at Geordie.

'Geordie Kinloch. I trained under you at Kleinfeld Neuhoffer a few years ago.'

'Ah yes, I remember you. You always laughed at my jokes.'

'I didn't know better then, although I admit I still occasionally use them. What are you up to these days?'

'I retired to the château in the Ardennes after my wife died. I shoot a bit around the estate and travel to visit my daughter, who lives in London.'

'Do you still invest the way you taught us? Sell in a rising market and buy in falling markets?'

'Good Lord, did I teach you that? As a matter of fact I recently sold everything. I couldn't stand owning a portfolio that looked so rich, even though my broker is recommending me to buy back the very stocks I have sold.' Chatel stood bolt upright with a twinkle in his eye. The old knight was in the saddle again. He paused, then added, 'Come to think of it, you should lead every part of your life that way, not just investing. Get out at high tide or the ebb will sweep you away.' He looked pensive. 'Yes, always leave the water before the tide turns.'

Geordie changed the subject. 'You said you did some shooting. If you ever come to Scotland we have some rough shooting you might enjoy. Pheasants, partridges, woodcock, snipe, some excellent pigeon woods.'

'I have a nephew at St Andrews University and I owe him a visit. I might just take you up on your offer.'

'Here's my card. Let me know when you plan to see your nephew. Bring him along too.' Geordie shook Chatel's hand. 'Unfortunately I need to get to a meeting at the Reform Club. It was a great pleasure seeing you again, Monsieur Chatel. Let me know when you come North.'

'Aristide. Call me Aristide now. We're not in the bank any more. I hope to see you again soon.'

Two months went by and the winter deepened in Scotland. Shortly before Christmas a letter arrived, written on the cream stationery of a

St James's club. Aristide Chatel intended to be in Scotland with his nephew for 'Hogmanay or some such pagan celebration' in a castle on the Black Isle and would like to take up the offer to 'perhaps shoot a haggis or two' – on his own – on the 4th or 5th of January.

Geordie called him and the date was set. He would arrive on the evening of the 3rd in time for dinner. Some rough shooting would be organized on the 4th; he would stay another night and leave after breakfast the following day to catch the ferry to Zeebrugge from Edinburgh.

The weather was whipping into a tempest by the late afternoon of January 3rd. The gale howled through the ancient avenues of beech at Balnadarg and the waning moon shone intermittently through the groaning branches and flurries of sleet. As the time of his arrival approached Geordie drove after dark to the lodge at the edge of his property in the Land Rover to clear fallen tree limbs and check whether any trunks lay across the drive. Several had come down in adjacent fields but none on the roadway. He waited at the lodge and could make out headlights a long way down the glen winking and vanishing with the twists and turns of the road. After fifteen minutes a green Bentley Mulsanne rounded the final corner and stopped behind the Land Rover. Geordie got out and staggered into the gale around to the driver's side. The window slid down and he saw Aristide's grinning face. 'A wild Scottish night. You live in a character-building climate, sir.'

'Good to see you, Aristide. Follow me and we'll be home in fifteen minutes.'

Geordie ran back to the Land Rover, jumped into the driver's seat and slammed the door, leaving the howling night outside. He switched up the heating and moved ahead as the sleet scored across the high beam. The slow convoy made its way through dense woodland and passed several impromptu waterfalls cascading off the rock face as they drove past. The road opened into landscaped parkland and the avenue of beeches. Shortly afterwards gravel crunched under their tyres as the vehicles pulled into a sheltered courtyard behind the castle.

Aristide swung out of the Bentley and held the top of the door to straighten his back, kinked after the long drive.

Geordie strode across the courtyard to greet him. 'Welcome to Balnadarg! Come inside and meet everyone. Stanley will take care of your luggage and lock your guns in the strongroom for the night.' A skinny man reached into the trunk to lift out two battered Louis Vuitton valises and a monogrammed leather gun case.

Geordie led the older man through the warm back corridor with its fishing nets, tennis racquets and golf clubs arrayed among old sporting prints and stuffed game birds mounted in glass cases on the walls. Waxed jackets, tweed caps and waders hung there on brass hooks. It smelled of gun oil, damp wool and dogs.

'This has a familiar ambience, Geordie. It reminds me of the gun room at the château.' The corridor ended in an oak-panelled hall with an iron wood burning stove glowing under the stone staircase.

Geordie introduced Aristide to his wife, Josie, and two small children peered over the banisters. 'Meet William my son and Emily my daughter. Hey, you should be in bed, you little monkeys.'

'Delighted to meet you, Josie. You are kind to have me to stay here.' He grinned at the children and popped his cheek, an unlikely gesture from the dapper old financier. They giggled and scuttled back along the landing to their bedrooms.

Josie welcomed her new guest. 'I've heard a lot about you, Aristide. How was your journey? Geordie, why don't you pour him a whisky and take him upstairs? You must be exhausted after your drive from the Black Isle. Why don't you take a bath, relax for an hour and we'll eat at nine o'clock.'

Aristide was installed in a warm room in the guest wing, shutters bolted and curtains drawn. Geordie turned on the bath taps and left him alone. Only the sound of rain slashing across the windowpanes and the occasional creak, rip and crash of nearby branches testified to the ferocity of the storm outside. Aristide placed his glass of Bowmore malt whisky carefully on a wicker chair beside the enormous bath, slipped into the steaming deep water and closed his eyes.

'I wonder what Balnadarg looks like in daylight. At least I sense that the ghosts here are happy.' He had fallen into the gentle habit of talking to himself since his wife died. As the warm water enveloped him he drifted around the turrets and into the courtyard, through the drawingroom, stairs and passages then finally into the wild night sky, where he swam through the clouds and saw the whole landscape in its craggy beauty. His wife flew beside him. She wore the same bun in her grey hair that she had worn since they were students at Louvain University in the 1950s. He always teased her because she looked like a loaf of bread. But how he loved that bread! How round, fair, fresh and fragrant it was. They held hands and swooped around the forests and battlements of Balnadarg.

A light knock on the door banished his reverie as Kinloch announced, 'Aristide – dinner will be ready in fifteen minutes.'

'Ah, very good. I will be down soon.'

He extracted the long plunger from the deep Victorian bath to release the water. He dried himself then donned tartan trews and a smoking jacket in honour of the occasion. He was downstairs in ten minutes.

Dinner was light and the conversation low-key. Kinloch saw that Aristide had aged but the puckish Belgian banker of his younger days was not far from the surface.

'I am always in my element when I go hunting. It's like the stock-market: you're pitted against people or nature, it's the same thing. A bird, a fox, a boar, a lawyer, a banker... I have to say they nearly always outwit me, but I always enjoy *La Chasse*. The occasional kill makes it worthwhile enough to keep you in the game.'

Kinloch enjoyed Chatel's modesty. He knew that the man had been a formidable player in his day and rarely lost.

'Do you still exit when the tide is flowing in your favour?' he asked.

'Of course. For that very reason, one day soon I expect to quit for good. You can be a great analyst but there is always an element of luck in investing. I have been lucky for a long time. Maybe too, I will have one final splendid day's shooting and hang up my guns for good. My nephew uses them when he comes to Belgium and I know he appreciates them. André Gide used to say that all objects – and people, for that matter – should belong to those who love them most.'

Josie cooed, 'I think that's beautiful, Aristide.'

He smiled. 'As a matter of fact I have had so much good fortune that I could check out right now. Sitting at this table I realize how fortunate I am with my friends. Can an evening like this be surpassed? A wonderful dinner in a warm castle, the best whisky, a jug of claret, a loaf of bread and a lovely lady.' He toasted Josie, who blushed at the hint of being compared with Omar Khayyam's object of desire.

'Aristide, it's past midnight and Johnnie the gamekeeper will be here at 8.15 in the morning. He's planned a full day for us tomorrow.' Geordie wanted to bring the night to a close before anyone got maudlin.

'Well, it's been a most enjoyable evening with fascinating company and great food. Many thanks for everything.'

'Do you want anything else before you turn in?'

'No, thank you; I have everything I need. Goodnight to you all.' With a smile and a slight bow, he left the dining-room in the direction of the guest wing.

Kinloch didn't know how well his guest shot but when Aristide opened his leather gun case after breakfast, it became clear. He saw an exquisite matched pair of sidelocked twenty-bores by the Belgian master gunsmiths Auguste Francotte. Geordie ran his fingers along the initials ARC damascened into the underside of the trigger guard.

'My grandfather Aristide was given them by his father as a wedding present in 1898. He gave them to my father as a wedding present in 1924. My father was killed by the Nazis in 1943. He never saw me getting married but I inherited them with everything else. They will go to my nephew.'

'The one in St Andrews?'

'Yes, Philippe is my only nephew. My brother's son. He's currently the youngest male Chatel, though judging by his success with the ladies I wouldn't be surprised to see new Chatels in the none too distant future.' As he spoke he assembled the two guns with a satisfying well-oiled click and slid them into sheepskin sleeves in preparation for the day's sport.

Johnnie was waiting in the courtyard with Minnie, his springer spaniel and Virgil, the family's over-excited black Labrador. Johnnie was a stocky Highlander with tightly cropped wiry gingery-grey hair. He wore a thick green tweed jacket, plus-fours and commando soled lace-up boots covered by canvas leggings. His handshake was surprisingly delicate, considering that his hands were torn and calloused from trapping foxes, erecting deer fences, cutting peat, handling heavy equipment, disembowelling red deer and the myriad other daily functions of a gamekeeper.

'I think we'll start with the teal in the flighting pond, surr. We'll leave the dogs in the Land Rover and walk quietly through the woods. We should take them by surprise. You'll have to be quick. They'll rise out of the pond rapidly and climb steeply until they're out of range to all but the luckiest shots.'

They cut across a beech wood carpeted with light snow until they saw a clearing. Johnnie motioned them to be very quiet and load the guns. Aristide slid the Francottes from their sleeves, instinctively peered up each barrel and loaded two cartridges into each gun, ran his finger along the safety catches, passed one to Johnnie and walked with the other.

They were on the outskirts of the clearing when eight teal rose out of the pond in a flurry of quacks and splashes. Aristide swung the shotgun and fired off two shots. One duck fell out of the sky and landed in the water with a dead splash, another crashed into a rhododendron behind the pond. Johnnie took the spent gun off him and passed back the loaded one.

By now the remaining birds had gained altitude and were almost out of range. Aristide fired two more shots. One teal bucked in the air but kept flying. Its companion was less fortunate and cartwheeled to the ground in a pile of feathers and fractured bones.

Johnnie let out an approving low whistle. 'Nice work, surr – nice work.'

This scene took about twenty seconds, during which Geordie managed to loose off two barrels from his elderly twelve-bore, hitting one bird and missing another.

'Some French partridges now. We need to drive to the next position.'

They returned to the castle through the woods and crammed into the Land Rover, windows steamed up by the excited dogs. Johnnie drove them half a mile along a muddy track then cut across a field to the base of a bluff capped by a crop of cabbages.

'Now, you two stand here thirty yards apart and I'll drive round with the dogs. Be ready for a good flush in about fifteen minutes.' Johnnie disappeared around the back of the hill while Aristide and Geordie deployed themselves as instructed.

The first sign of activity in the cabbage field was a flock of fieldfares and migrant finches disturbed from their feeding. They flew straight above the guns. These smaller birds were followed by alarmed cock pheasants, squeaking like rusty gates. They initially rose up towards the guns, then turned back and sailed downwind in the opposite direction. A squat grey partridge skimmed towards Aristide just above the cabbages and soared above as the ground fell away. He fired one shot and it fell on the stubble behind him, its red legs twitching for a few seconds as it gave up the ghost. Three more partridges came straight over, wings whirring. Geordie fired one shot and missed, as did Aristide, caught in the process of reloading.

Five partridges flew off to the left; there were four shots and three birds fell. There was a brief pause, followed by a flush of frightened partridges flying fast and high. Four shots and two birds landed with a thump like a falling handbag on the stubble. The dogs appeared on the brow of the hill, followed by Johnnie. He blew a whistle, signifying the end of the drive.

Aristide cracked his gun and grinned, 'Bless my soul, you need to be fast here. I'm not used to loading Old Francotte myself!'

'It's good for the character, Aristide.'

'*Oui*, Balnadarg is well set up for fast and high birds. I wasn't sure what to expect. You have excellent shooting here.'

The dogs ran around them, scenting and retrieving the mangled birds and delivering them excitedly to Johnnie. 'Not too bad, gentlemen. Six burrds for eleven shots.'

'Keeping score, are you, Johnnie?' Geordie ribbed him.

'Oh aye, I always keep score. I hope you're picking up your spent cartridges too. We don't want any of that pollution around here.'

The next port of call was a disused slate quarry. It was fairly shallow up to the rock face, which curved round like a horseshoe sixty yards across and rose a hundred feet in a vertical cliff of black, slimy rock. Johnnie walked with them to the foot of the cliff and found a large flat boulder on which he placed a canvas bag and a rug. He spread the rug and opened the bag. It contained a thermos of hot coffee, a thermos of game soup, some rolls and a flask of Whisky Mac.

'Now, you two can busy yerselves with this while I drive to the top. I'll beat the pheasants downwind, which is from right to left up there.' He described an arc with his arm across the rim of the quarry. 'The birds will be fast and up to sixty feet higher than the top of this cliff. Many good guns leave this place in despair,' he grinned, 'but if you give them a good swing and shoot well in front, you shouldn't have a problem. You might also see Belgian pigeons.' He watched a buzzard circling lazily above the crags, 'Don't hesitate to shoot them. Be in position in thirty minutes.' Jack scrambled down the loose rocks and disappeared out of the quarry.

'Belgian pigeons?' This was not a bird familiar to Aristide.

'The prosecutors tend to be more lenient if they think a foreigner shoots a protected bird in good faith. Buzzards are the pride of the bird protection lobby, but the bird lobby has no idea of the carnage wreaked by them on other birds and small mammals like the red squirrel. Johnnie reckons that at least thirty species are now endangered around here because buzzards are protected. Hence the need to thin out the Belgian pigeon population.'

'Come to think of it, they do look a bit like the crows we have in the Ardennes. We have a bounty on them, paid by the European taxpayer.'

'Johnnie will be pleased to hear that.'

The quarry was sheltered from the wind and the weak January sunshine played on their impromptu picnic table. There seemed something of the Hemingway about Aristide as he stood in his tweed suit drinking a Whisky Mac. He was a cracking good shot for a man of any age, let alone in his seventies. He was in his element but there was a distance about him, a wistfulness, which Kinloch attributed to their age gap. His wife had died, many of his friends were dead or incapacitated, his children grown up. It seemed to Kinloch that Aristide wanted to say something but could not. Suddenly he remembered the time, looked at his watch and snapped out of these thoughts. They had five minutes.

'Come on, Aristide, we need to get to battle stations.'

Kinloch positioned him at the base of the upwind cliff and moved forty yards to his left. Virtually as soon as they were in position, a cock pheasant zipped across the top of the quarry, its wings pinned back like a dart. It must have been travelling at fifty miles an hour a hundred feet above them. The speed and suddenness of the bird took Aristide by surprise and the shot he unleashed ripped the air six feet behind it. Kinloch had more time but his shot only removed a few tail feathers. The cock flew on, ruffled but alive.

Aristide rapidly got the measure of the quarry and was clipping pheasants left and right. Kinloch enjoyed watching his friend at the top of his art, but after watching many birds crashing lifeless against the cliff face, felt that the shooting had become too one-sided. They shot 27 pheasants and two 'Belgian pigeons' at the quarry, which Johnnie said was the best he had yet seen there.

As they walked back to the Land Rover he announced, 'Gentlemen, most unfortunately I must drive you back to the castle earlier than planned. I've just received a mobile message from the Department of Agriculture that needs to be dealt with immediately so I'm afraid I won't be able to take you shooting for woodcock today.'

'That's a shame.' Aristide was flushed with the number of pheasants he had just shot, and was ready to stay outside. 'Perhaps I'll get up early tomorrow and shoot a pair of woodcock to take back to Belgium.'

They were driven back to the castle and Josie had not yet returned from her errands. Kinloch showed Aristide around the walled garden and greenhouses, built a hundred years earlier and still functioning well, if expensively. Chatel inspected the seventeenth-century stables, expressing surprise that they were in a state of dereliction.

'They would make beautiful apartments. You're the big banker now. You could make a tidy sum if you converted and rented them. You should look at the numbers.'

'I have —and the loss of privacy is not worth the money.'

Aristide shrugged, then nodded his acceptance.

They took tea in the library, a masculine room with row upon row of ancient country books lining the walls on oak shelves from floor to ceiling. Aristide picked one at random, *Brown on Rural Affairs*, hoping for a salacious account of Life in the Shires, then opened the book at the chapter headed *'On the Management of Dung'*, and laughed at his misapprehension. He sat back in the deep Victorian armchair and rested his feet on Virgil's shiny black flank as he lay supine before the fire.

'Today is as close as I can imagine to a perfect day. I wake up in a deep warm bed in a Scottish castle and, after a hearty breakfast, am guided around your unspoiled countryside by an expert gamekeeper. The birds are as plentiful as in primeval times. The shooting is magnificent. We now sit in the library drinking perfumed China tea, leafing through books which have been on the same shelves they were put on two hundred years ago. Scotland has been involved in fifty wars since then and these gentle books wait to be picked up every twenty years or so, little gems reflecting the times in which they were written. You live in a peaceful haven, monsieur.'

'Yes, it's pretty peaceful here but it was not always thus. The Romans sent an expedition here, which was followed by a thousand years of internecine strife between tribes. This castle was a Jacobite stronghold and it was given a good pounding by the king's men in 1746. Many locals took up the wrong cause and were flogged, hanged or deported. A lot of sadness hangs over these glens. Many people think Scotland is the most haunted country on earth.'

'I feel that in the stones of Balnadarg. But some ghosts are happy ones; if I departed today I would be a happy ghost. I believe that a man should die at the peak of consciousness, the peak of happiness, the peak of strength. Waiting for the inexorable decline into incontinent old age is a miserable way to exit a great life.'

'Well, Aristide, you're still a long way away from that.'

'I wouldn't be so sure.' He smiled, adding, 'This would be a good moment. Sell at the top. It doesn't get better than this. Hey, what's that book ?' He got out of the chair and reached by tiptoe to a high shelf.

'Ah! *Beattie on Truth.* The certainty of the eighteenth century. What does he have to say? "*An Essay on the Nature and Immutability of TRUTH in opposition to sophistry and scepticism, by James Beattie LL.D., Professor of Moral Philosophy and Logic in the Marischal College and University of Aberdeen*". I love him already.' Aristide buried himself in the leather-bound volume for the next hour as Kinloch went about a few chores in his study.

The late afternoon sunshine slanted into the library and faded in a burst of spectacular colours over the western woods. Teacups were cleared, brass standard lamps switched on and curtains drawn. Kinloch placed three large beech logs on the fire. He broke the silence.

'My great-grandfather had evenings like this. He was an advocate and would sit in your very chair preparing cases for the local sheriff court. Sheep stealing was a prevalent crime back then. You were hanged or sent to Australia.'

'Which was worse?'

'Believe it or not, many pleaded to be hanged. Many never made it to Australia and very few returned. A surprising number of people like to know where they are going to be buried. Hanging gives you that certainty.'

Aristide laughed. 'That's for sure!'

'Tonight, we're going to have supper together as a family. The kids like guests. It gives them a reason to be on their best behaviour. I hope you don't mind. They go to bed at eight o'clock and we will eat at seven.'

'Charming. I look forward to it. I'd better go to my room and change into my best clothes for my dining companions.' He rose and stretched.

'We'll meet for drinks at 6.15 in the hall.'

'See you in an hour.'

Emily wore a red velvet dress and her blonde hair was braided like a little German girl's. She insisted on sitting beside Aristide because she had questions about Belgian chocolate. Her older brother William sat opposite, armed with questions about soccer if a gap opened in the conversation. He was a taciturn boy and quite happy to observe other peoples' conversations while he tucked into his dinner.

Warmed by a rich venison stew and a few glasses of claret Aristide sat at the table in a contented haze, teasing his pretty companion and asking William about his sporting interests. He was pleasantly tired and excused himself shortly after the children went to bed.

'Josie, Geordie, it's been a wonderful day. If you don't mind I would like to turn in now. My boat leaves tomorrow afternoon and I would love to walk around the woods in pursuit of some woodcock at first light. If I leave Balnadarg at eleven o'clock there should be plenty of time.'

'That should give more than enough time. I'm afraid that neither Johnnie nor I can come shooting with you. We have a business meeting in the morning. You can certainly take Virgil. He knows his way around here.'

'I'll look forward to that. Virgil and I will hunt together'. On hearing his name, a black tail lifted lazily a couple of times off the floor as the Labrador lay stretched in front of the fire. No other part moved. Aristide went to bed.

The next morning there was the usual bustle of a busy family preparing for the day. Everyone was in the kitchen and getting ready.

'Aristide, can I suggest that you take one of my guns this morning? You can put yours in the car ready for a quick departure and won't have to worry about cleaning them before you go.'

'That's a good idea. What are you offering?'

'Wait there.' Kinloch went to the strongroom and picked out a fine English twelve bore made in the 1920s which he thought his friend would appreciate.

'Take this. It shoots like a dream. Just watch the safety catch. It slides but doesn't click so you sometimes pull the trigger and nothing happens, or vice versa, which can be frustrating. I'll leave you a couple of boxes of cartridges and you're all set.'

Aristide cracked the gun and looked up the barrel. 'It feels light and comfortable. It'll do well, thank you.' He was done up in his tweeds and boots, ready for a morning's sport.

'You look every inch the Highland laird about to tour his estate. Now, to catch your woodcock, you need to cross the park in front of the castle. Go through the gate at the far end and take the track for about half a mile. You will come to a large plantation of young spruce and birch trees. If you walk noisily through there with Virgil, you will flush out some woodcock. I have to leave now. Take care of yourself and keep in touch.'

'I shall follow your instructions. I hope you will all visit me in the Ardennes. *Au revoir.*'

'We would love that. Drop Josie a line suggesting some dates. Goodbye – see you soon.' Geordie drove off.

Aristide patted Virgil, quivering with excitement. He emptied a box of cartridges into his jacket pocket and picked up the gun. 'Come Virgil, let's go hunting.'

They crossed the park pursued gently by five curious shaggy Highland cows. The sun's wintry rays slanted across the landscape through patches of mist and created a soft, soothing texture. Aside from footsteps crunching on the frosty grass, the cooing of pigeons and the cawing of a distant crow, there was complete silence in the still air.

They reached the edge of the plantation and Aristide stopped to load the gun. Virgil had already disappeared, a distant black tail wagging above the undergrowth marked his progress. An owl flew straight over and flitted silently into the woods behind. A mixed group of pheasants exploded indignantly in front of the dog and scattered left and right, well out of range of Aristide's gun. Besides, he was after woodcock, nothing else.

He pushed his way into the undergrowth, which was surprisingly heavy going. The ground was matted with dead willowherb and old tree stumps. It was impossible to keep a straight line and he panted loudly with the effort. He whistled for Virgil, but the dog was on his own mission, evidenced by the squeal of a rabbit forty yards away. He came to a clearing, propped the gun against a birch tree and sat on a mossy stump to catch his breath. The weak sunshine on his face felt good as he rested. It was clear that this adventure was going to take longer than Aristide anticipated, so he decided to abandon the quest for woodcock and return to the castle.

He gave several loud whistles. Virgil could be heard crackling and scrambling in the briar and emerged panting through a thicket into the clearing. He bounded forward enthusiastically when he saw

Aristide, knocking the gun off the birch tree. It fell heavily to the forest floor and exploded on impact. Aristide fell backwards against the tree stump, a ragged hole in the jacket above his belt.

'*Nom de dieu*, the dog has shot me.'

He was in momentary disbelief but purplish blood began to well through his clothes in unimaginable quantities. He tried stuffing a handkerchief into the wound to staunch the flow but was overwhelmed by pain.

'Must….lie back and think what to do …*que faire…*'

He was a mile from the castle and, for all he knew, many miles from the nearest person. Nobody would realize that anything was amiss until they found the Bentley later that afternoon. Virgil nudged him to get up, sensing that something was terribly wrong. It made no difference. Aristide couldn't move his legs and he began to drift. He could hope with futility that a passing stranger would find him in the next fifteen minutes. He knew that was impossible and that there were no further options.

Aristide floated above the downy birch trees. He drifted downwind like smoke, catching a glimpse of a broken figure on the forest floor being nuzzled by a distressed black dog. A gun lay on the ground. A solitary woodcock sailed across the clearing as the dark red orb of the sun slipped behind a bank of morning mist.

His wife gently took his arm and whispered, 'Aristide, you old rogue; you finally got out at high tide. You can come over now.'

Snitter and the New Meritocracy

to W. P. Young

Geordie Kinloch needed to assemble the cash equivalent of a town house to pay for his son's school fees. Out went the Indigo Blue V8 Morgan with beige Connolly leather seats. Out went the collected first editions of Kipling and Robert Graves. Out went the Scottish Colourist sketches. More insidious were the pleasures he had to forgo, such as the Alpine ski trips and the central heating when working alone in the house.

The sacrifice was worthwhile because his son William was blossoming at Cragside. He had a bunch of rascally, tousled friends, loved sports, played the bagpipes and was prospering academically. Kinloch always sensed that William would excel in anything he chose to specialize in. In the meantime he was a happy, popular all-rounder.

Geordie wrote to fourteen secondary schools to help the family decide where William would go to school after Cragside. He received prospectuses from famous old colleges around London to mid-sized public schools in the shires and more experimental establishments in Somerset and Scotland. One rainy Sunday morning he sat with his wife Josie at the kitchen table and they waded through a pile of brochures, prospectuses and application forms. After a pleasant couple of hours fantasizing about William at Winchester, Charterhouse or Eton, they agreed that Ambledean seemed to offer the best all-round fit for their darling son.

'I like the rural location and its stress on team sports,' said Geordie.

'It will be healthy for William to have girls at school. The music and acting facilities look great. I'd like to have gone there myself,' Josie approved.

Geordie called the Director of Admissions at Ambledean and arranged for a visit in the months ahead. They took William around the school and the day was a success. The application form was completed and a deposit sent off. William was offered a place at Ambledean in two years' time, conditional on an acceptable score in his Common Entrance exam and a reasonable headmaster's report from his prep school.

In June Geordie and his wife Josie went to meet Cragside's headmaster, Sebastian Mottram, for their annual one-on-one report on William's progress. Mottram had written that he wanted to discuss an idea for William's further schooling. They met in his snuff-scented study and sank into battered, all-encompassing brown armchairs.

The veteran headmaster pulled out a pale green file marked *Kinloch,* scanned it over his bifocal glasses and finally spoke, 'William's a solid pupil. He'll have no trouble getting through Common Entrance. He's a nice all-rounder. Where'd you say you wanted him to go?'

'He's going to Ambledean,' Josie replied.

'Ah, yes. Ambledean. A wonderful cricket school.' Mottram paused, took off his spectacles, affected a distant, thoughtful stare out of the leaded study window and turned back towards the Kinlochs. 'We've been thinking that William would be a strong candidate for The Snitter Institute, if you were ever to consider that option.'

'We didn't look at Snitter; we've really decided on Ambledean,' replied Josie, adding, 'Why do you think William would do well at Snitter?'

'Every June I confer with the senior teachers to select four or five boys to sit The Snitter Institute test the following autumn. It's considered an honour at Cragside to get on this list. There are usually about ten boys whose parents want them to sit the test each year, but we restrict the numbers. William's teachers think he's one of the strongest candidates this year.'

'Well, you're the one with the experience of Snitter. Why do you think William would do well there?' Josie repeated the question.

'He's a good all-rounder, academically sound, an athlete, musical. The sort of boy any school would be proud to have. Ambledean's an excellent school but you may think that a chance to pitch for a place at The Institute is worth taking. The worst that happens is that William ends up at Ambledean. It's a win, win.'

'Let's think about it. When do you need to know?' Kinloch asked.

'The beginning of next term.'

Kinloch was flattered by proxy, as it were, that his son was considered to be a strong candidate for The Institute. He'd known many Snits over the years and there was no doubt that the school gave a boy unusual self-confidence in preparation for the wide world.

As they drove down the glen in the evening sunshine from Cragside, the pair were silent for a while. Geordie broke the silence: 'If William has a chance to try for a place at The Snitter Institute he should go for it. He'll never regret sitting the test, whatever the outcome. He might regret not trying. I've worked with a lot of Snits and they do have the golden touch.'

'Why didn't you look at Snitter when you were getting all the prospectuses a few months ago?' Josie squinted in the sunshine as the car turned West.

'I had to draw the line somewhere. I wrote to fourteen schools and Snitter was number fifteen;' Geordie was dismissive.

'But why are you suddenly interested in it now?'

'Because Mottram seems to think William would do well there. It's like setting your sights on Ohio State and being told that you had a chance at Harvard University."

'That sounds a bit dubious – I think we should let sleeping dogs lie;' Josie was unconvinced. 'Willy's got a secure place at Ambledean so why stir things up? Besides, honey, we're really not Snitter parents. Look at you. You're all heavy brown brogues with clumps of mud on them. They're all Guccis and Aston Martins. That's not our crowd at all. Besides, I've also known a lot of Snits. They can be pretty full of themselves. I'm not impressed by many people I've met from that place.'

Over the summer Kinloch gradually persuaded Josie to lift her embargo on the idea. He also worked on William, who, because his father wouldn't leave him in peace, finally agreed to sit the test.

'If a boy has the opportunity to sit The Snitter Institute exam, it's an honour. More, it's *a sacred duty*, to answer the call,' he would pontificate to the nonplussed boy who typically looked up from what he was doing, say 'Whatever' and carry on as before.

Kinloch wrote to Sebastian Mottram to inform him of the decision. A week later, he received a letter from the Recorder of The Snitter Institute. It offered a selection of dates for William's test and suggested that parents might wish to accompany their sons for the day 'so that we can give you a full tour of The Institute while your son is undergoing his test and interview.' The date was set for the following October on the same day as another Cragside boy, Patrick Macaulay Reid.

It was a dank fog-filled autumn day when the two boys and their fathers met at a pub beside the river for lunch. The boys were out of place because they still had a Scottish glow in their cheeks, in contrast to the sallow, pimply youths milling around Snitter High Street at break time. The boys were nervous but still managed to pack away hearty plates of steak, peas and chips, followed by ice cream and washed down by ginger beer. The main topic of conversation between the fathers was that the outcome didn't matter but the challenge was worth it. Even to be selected by Cragside to get this far was a triumph.

Finally young Macaulay Reid slammed a spoon on the table and snapped, 'Dad, *will* you shut up about Snitter this, Snitter that? I'm here; I'm doing the Snitter test. I'll do my best, OK? If it's so unimportant, then shut up about it.'

The boy had evidently been badgered by his father about the subject as much as William Kinloch. Like his friend, he had a place assured at Ambledean and couldn't quite understand why he was being put up for the Snitter test if nobody cared about it.

After lunch they strolled up Snitter High Street, the boys jostling and pushing each other off the pavement in healthy horseplay. William put an arm around his friend, who was more nervous than he was. 'Hey, Patrick – they don't have girls here and you won't be able to roam in the heather and watch the skylarks and buzzards. In fact you won't be able to do anything. Snitter's just an island crammed between housing estates and a motorway.'

'Yes, but Dad went here – and his brothers, and their father, and *their* father.'

'So that makes it a good school, eh? My Dad didn't go there and he turned out all right. Actually he did a lot better than some Snits I can think of.'

He nudged Johnnie into the side of a phone booth. This was a cheeky reference to his father, Lord Macaulay Reid, a florid, charming peer famous for his love of whisky, who meandered affably along the pavement ten yards behind the boys.

'OK, boys, calm down. Straighten up. It's 2.20. We have to be at the Recorder's office in ten minutes.' Kinloch was getting twitchy.

They entered the imposing gates of The Snitter Institute. A passing boy directed them to the Classics Hall, an ivy-covered building at the far corner of an immaculate lawn. The four walked silently beside a wall skirting the lawn, carved with memorials to 'Snitter's Glorious Dead' from Trafalgar to Suez.

A kindly woman stood at the door to the Classics Hall with a clipboard. She ticked off the two names and ushered the boys inside. To the fathers, she said, 'Thank you, we'll take them now. You can get them back at six o'clock. Parental tours start at 2.45 in The Cobbles and run every 30 minutes after that.'

'The Cobbles?'

'Oh, that's the lawn over there. They took the cobbles up in 1790 and never got round to changing the name.'

'Oh...'

The Cragside boys looked robust compared to the gaggle of pallid, nervous candidates coming to be interviewed from suburban prep schools in Surrey and Buckinghamshire. One small boy wearing a 1950s era prep school uniform of short grey trousers, a purple blazer and pink tie went up to the clipboard lady, stuck out his hand to be shaken and said, 'How do you do? My name is Joseph Fendelburg and I am here for my interview.'

She ignored the proffered hand, smiled, ticked off his name and showed him through the door.

Another boy shook hands solemnly with his distinguished-looking Indian father who encouraged him, 'Do not forget, you are upholding the family honour, Jayantkhumar. Give it all your best.'

'Yes, sir,' the little boy with knobbly brown knees replied bravely.

'Well, Geordie, I have a few things I need to do for a couple of hours. I'm going to let you wander around the old Institute and I'll be back here around five.' Macaulay Reid had unfinished business in the pub by the river.

'Fine by me. I'll look around at my own pace. See you later.'

Kinloch decided to explore the school grounds and join a later tour. He walked down to the playing fields where inter-house rugby was being played on twelve pitches. Gaggles of supporters stood on the sidelines yelling arcane exhortations steeped in house history such as 'Remember Blenheim!' and 'Go Spartacus!'

The Institute Tree Game was also in motion. It was only played at Snitter because nobody else in the world could fathom it or relate to its traditions. From an outsider's perspective it looked like arboreal cricket, with eight boys positioned in various branches of an ancient oak tree and two boys chasing each other around the trunk. It was supposed to represent an incident in the Hundred Years War, and there was a ball involved.

Kinloch was getting cold in the sharp, moist wind. After trying to decipher the Tree Game for twenty minutes he returned to The Cobbles and picked up the next tour. He was in a group of twenty prospective Snitter parents and led around the college by a 'House Marm'. These redoubtable women were the backbone of Snitter's famed House system, responsible for controlling all domestic matters at The Snitter Institute. Kinloch's tour guide was impressive and it struck him that here was a lady well able to control a group of sixty pubescent boys.

After the parental tour Kinloch's group was ushered into a handsome Queen Anne building overlooking the playing fields. The plasterwork of the corridors and main hall was carved with the signatures of hundreds of former pupils. Kinloch was interested to see names which, over the centuries, subsequently won fame in battle, Parliament or just plain old-fashioned felony.

Rows of wooden wheel-backed classroom chairs filled the hall. They looked contemporary with the building and Kinloch wondered what dramas they had witnessed over the centuries. His group was directed to the front two rows just in front of a podium, behind which stood a sleekly groomed gentleman dressed like a head waiter. The parents sat down and the programme began.

'Good afternoon, Ladies and Gentlemen. My name is Ian Codrington, the Recorder of The Snitter Institute. To start things off I'd like to show you a short film about The Institute.' He clicked a button that activated a projector. Grainy old-fashioned footage was projected onto a screen behind him, accompanied by a sonorous voice.

'The Snitter Institute had humble beginnings as the Priory of St Teresa in the twelfth century. It was a teaching monastery, famous for producing illuminated manuscripts, including the St Teresa Psalter which can still be seen in the library today.' Medieval illuminations of the Four Seasons were shown on film, held gingerly by a senior boy in white gloves.

'The Priory was abolished at the time of Henry VIII but it received a charter to continue as a secular school. The school was initially called The Santer School, being an abbreviation of St Teresa, but this was soon considered too monastic in those anti-clerical times and its name was further corrupted to The Snitter School. It continued as a modest local school catering to the sons of local gentry for hundreds of years.

After the great educator George Thriepley became headmaster in 1823 it blossomed into one of the most successful English public schools, with over 500 pupils by the time he died in 1859. Under his leadership seven boarding houses were built, sports were incorporated into the daily routine of every boy and the use of corporate punishment mitigated to a maximum of ten lashes for serious wrongdoing. Its name was changed to The Snitter Institute in 1830, as a way of formalizing its position as the premier boarding school in Victorian England.

'The Institute's alumni include prime ministers, writers, musicians and adventurers. They also made their mark in the colonies, and today number several African leaders in addition to cabinet ministers in twelve countries.'

The film switched to 'Today's vibrant Snitter', which showed the usual compelling propaganda purveyed by every public school. There were shots of young men playing in the orchestra, positioning themselves in the Snitter Tree Game, rowing, playing Snitter Sevens, bell ringing and singing in the Victorian chapel. The film faded out with the rousing chorus of the Institute Song.

As the spine-tingling music faded, Codrington took the podium. 'Thank you, ladies and gentlemen. I hope you enjoyed that brief introduction to The Snitter Institute. You will probably want to know the process by which we select boys for entry to The Institute.' The Recorder slowly surveyed the expectant faces of his audience. 'Until a few years ago it was necessary to put a boy's name down at birth and, subject to reasonable Common Entrance scores at 13 and an acceptable headmaster's report from the boy's prep school, the boy usually got in. Today, with pressure from School League Tables and a political climate demanding more *social justice* and, er, *meritocracy*, we have devised an arm's-length, objective test designed to screen for the kind of pupils we believe should attend The Snitter Institute in the future. Of course, I am not at liberty to disclose the exact nature of the test, but can assure you that it cannot be prepared for. It's a computer interface that looks for linguistic and mathematical aptitude through verbal and non-verbal testing, and was specially commissioned from a panel of educational psychologists by the Institute's Court.

'The test, however, is just part of the picture. We conduct a thorough interview of the boy to get a sense of how well-rounded he is. We look for non-academic talents which would contribute to the community of the Institute if he were to join us. Are there any questions so far? Yes, sir – over on my right?'

The distinguished Indian gentleman stood up.

'Thank you, Mr Codrington. You are asserting that you have radically different criteria for selection than in the old days. Can you confirm that registration at birth is no longer important? Do you rely entirely on ten-year-old boys being put up by their prep schools for your annual intake?'

'That is largely correct. But it would be inaccurate to say that long standing registration is completely unimportant. If parents register their children at a young age, we usually get to know the parents and the child as he grows up, which helps in our understanding of the child, but he will still need to go through our testing and interview programme. If he fails to impress there, he won't get in.'

'Thank you very much.' The Indian gentleman sat down.

'After a day of tests and interviews followed by a three-week assessment period by the panel of staff and psychologists chaired by the Headmaster, the results are split into three categories. We offer boys a place subject to achieving the required score in the Common Entrance exam at the age of 13; we put them on a waiting list or we turn them down altogether.

'Not all boys who are offered a place will accept, which means that boys on the waiting list will have a good chance of eventually getting a place at The Institute. Boys turned down altogether will not be part of this process and will not be asked to proceed. I should stress that boys in the third category are not bad, but we feel that they simply don't fit the Snitter mould. Some have gone on to become quite successful at other schools, but by and large we remain highly confident of our process. Our testing process is completely meritocratic.' Codrington touchingly found it hard to conceive how anyone not attending The Snitter Institute could be a success in life.

'Now, if there are no more questions, I would like to invite you to have some tea and biscuits downstairs. You can mingle with members of Staff while you're waiting for your boys to come out of the testing area. Please use this opportunity to ask any questions.'

There was an exodus from the hall along a corridor and downstairs into a splendid vaulted basement. Portraits of ancient Snit worthies adorned the walls, forgotten generals and scholars in equal measure.

Gradually the young boys began to enter the room in twos and threes and made for their parents like lambs to their mothers. They were debriefed anxiously.

Patrick Macaulay Reid was almost in tears. 'I couldn't finish the test and didn't do well on the questions that I did finish. The interviewer didn't like me and the whole thing was a disaster.'

His father, having recently re-emerged from his afternoon's business, patted the boy affectionately on the back, proclaiming loudly, 'Couldn't matter less, dear boy, couldn't matter less.'

Kinloch overheard similar tales of distress from other boys bleating to their parents, so expected the worst from William. But when he entered the hall, he was remarkably relaxed. He confided to his father in a matter-of-fact way, 'The computer interface was not very sophisticated but the test was well structured. Dad, there are three things I don't like about Snitter Institute: they don't have girls here, you can never get away from the sound of the motorway and the teachers are incredibly pompous.'

'Willy, it's never wise to be too open with your feelings at times like this. But you do have a point,' Kinloch replied in a whisper, taken aback at his son's observing the emperor's lack of clothes.

He had been struck himself that afternoon by the proximity of the motorway. While watching the Tree Match he thought how sad it was that Snitter's dreaming spires were so compromised by the orbital transport system.

'Dad, I really would like to talk to you about all this – in private, if you like.' William tugged his father's arm.

At that moment a tall, youngish man with prematurely grey backswept hair entered the Hall. He wore a loud pinstripe suit of the sort that upper end life assurance salesmen wore in the 1970s. Macaulay Reid let out a low whistle and uttered in a stage whisper, 'Hey Kinloch, look at those amazing threads!'

Kinloch nudged him. 'That's the Headmaster, Peter Edgeware.'

'Oops!' Kinloch smelled the whisky on his friend's breath.

Codrington escorted the Headmaster around groups of parents. When he came to the small Cragside group he confided he didn't know Scotland well but hoped that The Snitter Institute would develop more of a franchise there. He asked young William how his day had gone, and the boy replied shyly, 'I'm glad it's over.'

Peter Edgeware was metropolitan and limp. Kinloch couldn't imagine him on the back of a tractor or up a Munro in the Highlands. He bore no resemblance to the muscular educationalists of his youth. He thought of H. R. McLeod, his old school pastor, who had been a chaplain in the Cameron Highlanders at Ypres. He looked at Ian Codrington to his left and Peter Edgeware on his right, as smooth as head waiters in an overpriced restaurant. He thought of Major Gilbert, his modest old maths teacher, who had won the DSO for destroying a German machine-gun nest at Monte Cassino. He could hear Major Gilbert asking, 'Do you really want your son in the hands of these men, Geordie?'

It was with relief that they gathered up their coats and spilled into the damp, darkening evening air. William pulled his father ahead on the pavement and said, 'Dad, I really need to talk to you.'

'Fire away, Tiger.'

'Dad, I don't know how I did in the Snitter test, but I don't like this place and I don't belong here.'

'Why's that, Willy?'

'As I said before, I want to be at school with girls, and I hate the sound of the motorway all the time. I want to go to school in the country, where you can breathe. And I really didn't like the man who interviewed me; he was so pompous. Why do they wear such ridiculous clothes?'

'Here's my suggestion. Let's go out for a nice Chinese meal and have a really good talk about all these things.'

'Good deal, Dad.'

Two weeks later a letter arrived at Balnadarg with a southern postmark.

Dear Mr and Mrs Kinloch,

It is with regret that we are unable to offer your son a place at The Snitter Institute. We considered all the information available to us and concluded that his claims were not as strong as those of some other boys.

The Head of your son's current school is being advised and will, no doubt, be able to discuss alternative schools with you for your son.

Yours sincerely,

Peter Edgeware

Headmaster.

Kinloch stared at the letter for a long time. He wondered what information had enabled The Snitter Institute to conclude that William's claims were not as strong as some other boys. What a strange expression. Did they know about Willy's collection of rocks from around the world, carefully labelled and catalogued? Did they know about his amazing empathy for animals? His computer skills? His photographic memory for the books he had read? Did they know he was the regional Under 11 discus-throwing champion? That he could list every song recorded by Jimi Hendrix in chronological order, from memory? That he could play twelve tunes on the bagpipes?

Those southern prep schools were clearly better at grooming their boys than the free-spirited Cragside, but Snitter had failed to spot a true gem.

'Oh well, bugger Snitter,' Kinloch said to nobody in particular and rose out of his chair. He called Macaulay Reid, who picked up the phone immediately.

'Ah, Kinloch, old sport. Good news! Patrick made it into Snitter. I take it that William sailed in?'

'He didn't even make it to the waiting list.'

'That's very odd.' He paused, then resuming his jolly tone, 'Oh well, back to Ambledean, eh?'

'Back to Ambledean, indeed.'

'Ciao then – I'm on the other line. We'll catch up over a drink soon.'

'Sounds great. 'Bye.'

So the Honourable Patrick Macaulay Reid found a spot with his ancestors.

A month later Kinloch was in the kitchen and overheard William in the room next door boasting to a visiting group of friends, 'I flunked the Snitter Test.' He spoke as if it were a badge of honour, a wound stripe. He made it seem heroic to have been rejected by The Institute. His friends laughed with admiration.

It struck Kinloch like lightning. Pushing for William to get into Snitter had been his agenda, and his alone. Neither William, nor Josie, nor their friends could understand his interest in the ageing restaurant with its head waiters decreeing that this boy pass, that boy fail. There was nothing relevant in the Snitter proposition to an exceptional boy like William. Kinloch had allowed himself to be seduced into a socio-educational honey trap and he felt very foolish for the experience.

The boys all looked astounded when Kinloch entered the room with a bottle of Veuve Clicquot and seven glasses. He put the tray down and flicked off the television programme they were watching.

'I think you're old enough to try champagne.'

He put his arm around his son's shoulder and toasted: 'Here's to the best boy on the block!'

The Big Smoke

to Bill Daniels

They were mellow with malt whisky and Highland dancing when they spilled out into the chilly star-spotted mountain night. Josie hugged the shawl tightly over her long dress as they walked the few paces to the frozen old Jaguar. The noise of reel music bravely trying to keep up with the disintegrating night could be heard pounding through the walls of the village hall, interlaced with tribal yelps and breaking glass. The engine coughed, then rumbled to life in a cloud of fumes. Geordie let it gurgle to let some heat circulate around the car, eased up the clutch and headed down the rutted track.

The old glen road was tortuous but easy to negotiate at night because corners could be cut if no lights were coming from the opposite direction. Geordie couldn't remember the last time he met another vehicle on this narrow road at night, which was why he drove at a more careless speed than his condition warranted.

'Slow down, honey. Watch out for the roe deer. You often see them on the road at night.' Josie tried to persuade her husband to slow down in a manner that wouldn't impugn his virility or driving skills.

'I *am* watching out,' he retorted as he swung the car around a corner into a cutting with steep banks and no shoulder. He accelerated into the corner because he knew the road so well. It straightened into a long fast stretch and he was ready to let the old car rip. That night, however, as he pulled into the straight, there was a large white rounded object lying directly in his path.

'Look out!' shouted Josie as Kinloch slammed on the brakes and skidded wildly. The car missed the obstruction but was careening along so fast that it shot up the embankment on the left, tipped and rolled over twice before landing the right way up on the roadway sixty yards beyond. By some quirk of physics the car ended up facing the way it had just come. The headlights pointed hazily at a large white sack on the road, which loomed impassively through a cloud of exhaust and dust like a zeppelin caught in enemy searchlights.

There was a momentary silence.

'Great balls of fire. Josie, are you all right?' In the turbulence the car's interior lights had switched on and Kinloch saw the shock and disbelief in his wife's face.

'Get me out of this thing *now!*' she commanded. She was shaking and couldn't summon the force to open her door.

'All right. Don't move'. He pushed open the driver's door and it fell off its severed hinges onto the road. He made his way unsteadily around to the passenger side and pulled open Josie's twisted door, to the sound of scraping metal. He helped her out of the seat and she stood shakily on the roadside.

'You all right? I'm so sorry.'

'And you're drunk, so we can't call anyone. If we do, the police will get you. Not only that, we're ten miles from home and five miles from the nearest house.' Kinloch wasn't sure if his wife was shaking from shock, cold or anger. He pulled an old tartan rug from the car's back seat and threw it over her shoulders.

'Stay there and I'll see if I can get the car to move.' He looked around the battered Jaguar and could see, in the limited light, that there didn't seem to be anything structurally wrong. The tyres were sound, nothing was hanging off the underside and the engine wasn't staved in. The windows were intact, except for the driver's door, which lay forlornly on the road

He turned the ignition key and the engine started. He depressed the fateful accelerator pedal, slipped into first gear and engaged the clutch. The car lurched forward with a grinding sound.

'At least it moves. I think I can get this thing home.' He left the engine on and helped Josie back into the car. He heaved the broken door onto the back seat.

'I'm going to have a look at that bloody sack.' Kinloch drove slowly towards the cause of their accident. He got out to inspect the mysterious plastic bag. It was sealed and undamaged. A printed label was stitched on the polythene.

> *WARNING. Cannabis is designated under Section 7(4) of*
> *the Misuse of Drugs Act 1971. Seeds may only be planted*
> *under strict licence from the Home Secretary.*
> *75 kg Tiborszakkasi cannabis seed. Authorized use only.*

'Holy cow, Josie, this is dope! Seventy-five kilos of cannabis seed. I'm going to shove it into the boot before someone misses it and comes looking for it. Home Secretary, my arse.'

'For heaven's sake, Geordie, let's go home. If the police stop us, the car's unfit for driving, you're drunk and now you want to carry 75 kilos of cannabis seed in the boot. Are you quite mad?'

'I can explain, officer. Honest.' He grinned. She looked at his bow tie, untied and hanging dishevelled down the front of his oil-stained dress shirt. One sleeve of his velvet blue smoking jacket was almost detached, as was one leg of those bespoke tartan trews she gave him for his birthday many years ago. There were oil smudges across his face. But miraculously, he was unhurt, and she could only smile as her overgrown schoolboy was about to hijack a sack of illegal seed.

After a lot of heaving and grunting he manoeuvred the sack and finally tipped it into the boot. He slammed down the lid and drove off not much faster than walking pace, the heater blowing valiantly to compensate for the lack of a passenger door. His trophy made him strangely oblivious to the fact that he had just wrecked his car and nearly orphaned his children.

In the morning Kinloch awoke in a cloud of biliousness. He sat on the edge of the bed and cradled his pounding head in his hands. 'Why don't I ever bloody well learn? ....Why do I still do this to myself?'

Josie still slept. Seeing his tattered formal clothes strewn across the floor, he tried to put together his last few waking hours. Vaguely hoping it was but a feverish dream, he staggered to the lavatory and peered into the courtyard. The dear old Jaguar looked like a wrecked circus car. The roof had a deep gash running front to back between the passenger seat and the driver, as if punched and ripped by a giant can opener. He could see the car seats clearly through the torn metal. Six inches to the left or right and someone would have been killed last night. The driver's door was missing, bodywork on both sides was gashed, scratched and ragged. The front and back were surprisingly undamaged, but the car was definitely a write-off.

Kinloch filled a whisky tumbler with water and dropped in two Alka Seltzer tablets. The fizzing sound as they dissolved was painfully loud. Grasping the tumbler he made his way tentatively downstairs into the courtyard. He shuffled around the mutilated body of his Jaguar like a sad mourner filing past an open coffin. When he reached the boot, he prised it open. The large white sack still lay there like a beached whale, its label winking at him: *WARNING. Cannabis is designated under section 7(4) of the Misuse of Drugs Act 1971…*

He began to feel more robust as the Alka Seltzer worked its relief through his vital parts, patted the sack, shut the boot and went to the kitchen to call Johnnie, the gamekeeper.

'Hi, Johnnie – if you have a moment today I wonder if you could come round. I would like to chat about something with you.'

Johnnie arrived an hour later in his working tweeds. The highlander had a serious, professional manner about him, but there was always a twinkle in his blue eyes ready to ignite into a broad crease of laughter at the slightest provocation. As soon as he saw the wreck in the courtyard, he whistled. 'I see the missus had trouble competing for a parking space at the supermarket this morning.'

'It was me, actually. Lucky to be still in one piece. But take a look at this.' Kinloch showed him the contents of the open boot.

Johnnie looked at him and whistled again. 'Seventy-five kilos of cannabis seed. Ye're dealing now, are ye?' Johnnie laughed. He read out the printed label, stitched on the plastic, '*Designated under Section 7(4) of the Misuse of Drugs Act 1971*. Very interesting.'

'It was lying in the middle of the glen road at one o'clock this morning. I came around the corner at speed and I could either plough straight into this thing, or take evasive action. Ended up rolling the car down an embankment, but we finished the right way up. I took it with me as a souvenir.'

'So what are ye goin' to do with it?'

'I thought you might have some ideas. Seems a shame to waste it.'

Josie quietly appeared in the courtyard while the men were talking. 'My idea is to get rid of the bag immediately. Put it back on the roadside and let the owner find it.'

'Right enough, I heard that old Kenny Fleming up the glens has a deal with a pharmaceutical company to produce cannabis under licence, for medicinal purposes, as they say. He'll have hell to pay for losing this bag.'

'He shouldn't be so careless, Johnnie. Besides, it nearly cost me my life. I think *we* should plant it – for experimental purposes. I can always say the label got detached and we planted the seeds just to see what came up. A mystery bag of seeds that fell off the back of a lorry. Nobody could get you for that.'

'Right enough, surr. Where d'ye want to plant them?'

'I thought we could take the north-east corner of Hatton Field. It's been in set aside for five years; it's in the heart of the estate, surrounded by woodland, no pathways anywhere close, not visible from any road. If anyone official comes across it we can tell them we found a bag of seed – which is true – and planted it to attract wild birds.'

'Aye, the partridges will fly high on this stuff, right enough,' added Johnnie with a chuckle. He then looked hard at Kinloch. 'But what *are* ye going to do with it, surr?'

'We'll tell them what I've just said. But between you and me, it's an experiment. If it flourishes maybe we can get a licence from the Home Office to grow some next year. No point going through all the bureaucratic hoops only to find it doesn't grow well on this farm, is there? A pilot scheme, you might say.'

Johnnie reflected for a while before speaking, 'OK, surr, on the understanding that it's wild bird seed I'll help ye plough up and drill one acre on the north-east corner of Hatton Field this afternoon.' Johnnie was in. The Alka Seltzer had soothed Kinloch's head and he was starting to feel his usual chipper self again. Josie shook her head and carried on with her morning errands.

'Good lad. Not a word to anyone, now.'

'Not a word.'

It was late May and the peaty soil received the vibrant seeds in its moist vernal womb. They germinated quickly and very soon there was a vigorous green fuzz over the sown area. Johnnie sowed the seeds at twice the recommended density, arguing that half a hectare was quite enough to establish whether cannabis would grow on this farm or not. Also, dense sowing was compatible with the wild bird seed mix they could claim they were officially planting.

In six weeks the crop was twelve inches high and as dense as a carpet. Kinloch recognized the leaves from his university days, when his flatmate grew cannabis in the bathroom under intense artificial light enhanced by silver foil tacked to the walls and ceiling. These leaves looked like a cross between a maple leaf and a nettle. He wondered if it was time to test the crop.

He called Johnnie. 'D'you think it's time to sample our wild bird seed crop in Hatton Field? Shall we meet there at two o'clock this afternoon?'

'Aye, surr, see you there.'

They walked slowly around the plot. There was some damage around the margins, where rabbits ventured out of the woods and grazed at night. Also quite a lot of plants had been topped carelessly, stripped and ripped by passing roe deer. 'I wonder what the deer feel like after grazing on this stuff?' mused Johnnie.

They both spotted it simultaneously and the conversation stopped dead. A rectangular patch of cannabis had been trimmed neatly down to the ground and the stalks removed.

'Whoa, Johnnie. Who d'you think did that? They've taken two or three kilos of the stuff. Do you think the police took a sample?'

'No. They're less subtle than that. Ye'd be explaining your farming practices in police custody,' replied Johnnie.

'Could it be someone from the Farming Executive?'

'The Executive? No, they'd take one square metre crop samples from several locations in the field.' Johnnie fetched his lumberman's tape from the Land Rover and measured. 'This isn't metric. It's exactly six by three feet. The Farming Executive are particular that way. If they don't follow exact metric guidelines from Brussels, they don't get paid.'

'So it's nobody official?'

'Probably not, though you can't rule out that someone else took a sample for analysis.' Johnnie knelt and inspected the cut stalks. 'Cut recently. In the last 24 hours, I'd say. A sharp tool. Secateurs, probably, or a machete.'

'Told anyone, Johnnie?'

Johnnie looked in Kinloch's eyes squarely and arched an eyebrow, 'Not a soul, surr. Not a soul.'

'Hmm. Must be one of those ramblers, exercising their Right to Roam.'

'The Right to Stagger, I'd say, after smoking this stuff,' Johnnie added. He agreed to keep a close watch on the site over the next few days. He was a professional stalker and seemed to love nothing more than lying motionless for hours in a wet ditch, observing activities on the forest floor. Kinloch remembered his father telling stories about stalkers from Highland estates being recruited as snipers during the war. Johnnie's infinite patience and his owl's eye for the slightest movement would have qualified him to be a lethal sniper in the rubble of France or the jungles of Burma.

The next morning at 8 o'clock, Johnnie called Kinloch from his mobile phone. 'Ye're not going to believe this, Geordie. At 1 o'clock this morning Rory Dallas took a bag-load of cannabis leaves from the field.'

'Was he alone?'

'Aye.'

'Was he in uniform?'

'No – waxed jacket and a flat cap.'

'Was he in the police car?'

'No – his old Vauxhall.'

'Well, I'll be damned. How much did he take?'

'One black polythene bagful. About the same as last time.'

'Personal or official use, do you think, Johnnie?'

'Hard to tell, but I've heard it said that he's partial to the odd smoke.'

'Better terminate this conversation on the mobile. Come round for breakfast.'

Twenty minutes later Johnnie was sitting in the kitchen with a mug of tea, warming his feet by the wood burning stove.

'So what do ye make of this, surr?'

'I've no doubt that he knows what it is. Rory was in the Drug Squad in the Eighties. The real question is, is he cropping our field for personal use or is he getting tests done?'

'I think I have your answer. After Rory left the field, I waited twenty minutes then followed him home. I parked in the wood by his driveway and walked along the bank of the river opposite his house to get a better view. I saw him coming out of his fish smoking hut.'

'Did he see you?'

'No. But when he returned inside his house and the lights went out I crossed the river and inspected the hut. It took ten minutes to pick the padlock, and I have to say I got twitchy. Their dog was barking inside the house and wouldn't shut up. At one point I saw lights go on, but nobody came out.'

'So you got into the hut?'

'Aye. Rows of marijuana stalks quietly drying in the racks like kippers. Must have been ten kilos of weed at various stages of preparation.'

'No evidence of analysis or research?'

Johnnie laughed. 'No, surr – one hundred percent social, domestic and pleasure.'

'Looks like I need to pay a visit to our local bobby. I suspect we have scope for negotiation. Tell me, Johnnie, how on earth do you think he found the stuff in the first place?'

'Ye'd be amazed at the people ye find rambling across the estate at odd times of day and night. Maybe he was walking his dog and just stumbled across the plantation. He would know that it wasn't authorized. The police have a list of all licensed growers in the area and you're not one of them. Home Office Regulations are pretty tight on this one.'

'Intrusive bastards.'

'Aye, well, that's the way it is, surr.'

'I think my next port of call is to visit PC Dallas.'

PC Rory Dallas was well known in the glens. He knew of every ceilidh, celebration and impromptu party that was taking place and for the past twenty years had made it clear discreetly that if everybody played the game, so would he. Playing the game in these parts meant being sensible when drunk. He wouldn't be on the lookout for erratic driving, but would come down with all the force of the law if a drunk driver was involved in an incident.

He hated to clog the court system with petty crimes. If a youth was reported stealing a CD from a schoolmate or strawberries from a neighbour's garden, PC Dallas would show up on his doorstep and negotiate reparation from pocket money or in the form of weeding the neighbour's garden. The matter would conclude there and then – no criminal record, no paperwork, no tax-funded court case; the whole cumbersome apparatus of overpaid bureaucrats in overheated offices trickling Social Justice down to the masses was bypassed by the common sense of PC Dallas. His *modus operandi* was simple, fair and to the point. His beat in the glens had the lowest reported per capita crime rate in the British Isles.

'Anyone home?' Kinloch stuck his head around the half-open front door. A young brindled Staffordshire Bull Terrier came skidding out of the kitchen, picked up speed along the passageway and launched itself into his arms. He caught the pup whereupon she piddled down his shirt with excitement and tried to lick his face. There was no sign of an owner, so Kinloch walked back into the garden and around the house, led by the exuberant puppy. He followed her along a gravel path flanked by a well-groomed lawn down to the river, at the end of which was a hut built like a miniature Swiss chalet. This was PC Dallas' famous fish smoking hut.

The bull terrier barrelled against the quaintly stencilled door of the hut and it burst open with a bang. Various expletives issued from within. Geordie was hard on her heels and saw the rows of drying marijuana stalks which Johnnie had described earlier. He quickly averted his gaze and, pretending not to have noticed, suggested, 'I was just passing by, Rory. Got time for a quick coffee?'

'Er… yes. Yes, of course. Coffee. Great idea.'

The flustered policeman swiftly closed the door of his hut and led the way back up the path to the lodge.

'A very long time no see, Geordie. To what do I owe the pleasure?' He looked back at his hut furtively, seeming reassured that the door had not sprung open to reveal his hobby to the world. They entered the house and sat at the kitchen table.

'Rory, hope I'm not disturbing you. I want your advice.'

'Shoot, Geordie.'

'I'll get straight to the point. A couple of months ago I was driving along the glen road at night and narrowly avoided killing Josie and myself while steering past a bloody great sack of cannabis seed lying in the middle of the road. In part exchange for writing off my dear old Jag I took the sack with me. I planted the seed in a remote corner of the farm as 'wild bird seed' on a hidden piece of set aside land surrounded by trees. About half a hectare.'

The kettle boiled furiously and clicked off. PC Rory Dallas shook instant coffee from a jar into two mugs and poured the seething water on top. He mopped up a small spill, went to the fridge and poured milk into a jug. It seemed to Kinloch he was trying to mask his nerves by faffing around in the kitchen.

'You know that's an offence, don't you?' His instinctive officiousness came to the fore.

'The way I describe it, yes. But if it came to that I would deny that I knew it was cannabis. Just a sack of seeds with the label missing. Easily detached, any court would agree. We planted it out of curiosity to attract wild birds. I'm confident that I could talk my way out of a jail term. My crime would be diminished to not reporting that I had found a bag of seed. Is that a crime? I think I was doing a public service by moving a heavy object obstructing the queen's highway. No? Anyhow, by some magic means, word is getting out. There are already some midnight harvesters snipping away at the edges of my wild bird plants.'

'So why are you telling me, Geordie?'

'Personally I don't care for drugs, but am adamantly against government interference in our lives. If a man wants to inhale on a piece of smouldering vegetation, that's entirely his business. Prohibition criminalizes normal and often quite harmless activities. It makes the wrong people rich and costs taxpayers billions in fruitless policing costs. I can't think of one example in history of a successful prohibition. Can you, Rory?'

'Not offhand. I'm still unclear where you're going with all this, Geordie.' PC Dallas looked increasingly uncomfortable.

'Where I'm going is that I assume this will go no further because we're on the same side.'

'So you know?'

'So I know? Oh come on, Rory. You were spotted taking cuttings from the field last night, and your smoking hut speaks for itself. Matter of interest, how did you find out about my field?'

'Kenny Fleming in the glens reported the loss of a 75 kilo bag of cannabis seed a few weeks ago. He's the only farmer registered to grow it in this area. I've been looking around local farms and came across your plantation last week.' Now it was in the open, the wily old policeman relaxed visibly. He tapped his nose and grinned, 'Besides, I've got a nose for unusual crops.'

'Fair enough. Your secret is safe with me.' Kinloch swilled down the dregs of his coffee and rose from the kitchen table.

'And yours with me. I would suggest, though, that you burn the field and plough it in as soon as possible before the word gets around to the wrong people. You certainly don't want the law hearing about this – it might get complicated. Thanks for your visit. Oh and Geordie, I appreciate your discretion in this matter.'

'Any time, old chap.'

Campbell was a huge red-haired Scotsman, straight out of Central Casting. His hands were swollen from heavy drinking and repairing dry stone dykes without gloves in all weathers. He had a heart of gold and would only flatten a man for good cause, which tended to occur most Friday nights after a quiet ten pints at the Reid Arms in the village of Invermore. Being a model citizen he would then leave his car in the village and walk home across country, the directness of his route being determined largely by the volume of alcohol swilling around his system.

Campbell woke up in the north-east corner of Hatton Field one morning in late June. He staggered across to a drainage ditch and plunged his head into the cold muddy water, which woke him up. He saw an unfamiliar plant growing, which bore a resemblance to the stuff that his GP, Dr Mackenzie, somewhat unofficially recommended he should substitute for alcohol. He told his GP it would be a sad day when he could no longer drink beer and whisky, but Dr Mackenzie counselled him to try cannabis 'To preserve what's left of your liver. And you won't get a hangover.'

PC Dallas had helped him out of the pub the previous evening and sat him on a bench in the village square, lecturing him, 'You're getting too old for this game, Campbell. Take a quiet hint from me. Find your way to Hatton Field and try some softer stuff. It won't make you fight, damage your liver or affect your weight.' The fact that it might cause advanced paranoia in later life was a safe bet for Campbell. His chances of living into old age were not high.

Dimly recalling the encounter, Campbell scratched his thick, tousled, grass-filled, matted red hair and muttered, 'Did Rory Dallas tell me to come here? Fokked if I know. Oh, well!' – whereupon he stuffed his checked lumberman's shirt with cannabis leaves. 'I'll hang it o'er the wood burning stove and try it when it gets dry; then I'll never again have a hangover like this one. Never again.'

The property adjacent to Kinloch's farm was an ancient estate, the relic of a royal land grant in the twelfth century to a family descended from an ancient line of Pictish kings. It was once a kingdom which straddled much of what later became known as Central Scotland, but the inexorable erosion of family resources by two thousand years of fighting the Romans and Vikings, court intrigues, Oliver Cromwell, dubious marriages, Jacobites, two world wars, inheritance taxes and New Labour had whittled it down to a mere 24,000 acres of mixed farmland and a grouse moor. The current incumbent was the 37th Earl of Mormaer and a more charming, earthy character it would be hard to meet. He was known universally as Jock the Earl – pronounced *Errol* by the locals – and lived in Mormaer Castle, a vast haunted crenellated pile with origins in the eighth century.

The Earls of Mormaer had occupied a seat in the House of Lords and contributed to British public life for nearly a thousand years. In a triumph for social justice the Earldom's entitlement to a seat in the

Lords came to an abrupt end under New Labour's reforms. Jock was thus at a loose end so often went to his local pub, the *Mormaer Arms*, for meals, a few drinks and a chat with any tenants who happened to be there.

He was sitting quietly at a table in the bar one lunchtime reading a tabloid newspaper when Campbell entered. He threw down the paper and welcomed his companion.

'Hey, Campbell – come and sit down. Let me buy you a whisky.'

He sat beside his old friend and confided, 'I'm off the booze, but I'd take a ginger beer if yer offer's still good, Jock.'

'Good Lord, Campbell, of course the offer's still good. What happened?'

'Jock, the reason I'm here today is to say I won't be coming doon to the pub any more. Dr Mackenzie says I'm killin' myself wi' alcohol, so I've found something else.'

Jock looked quizzically at Campbell. They'd drunk together for twenty years, been on adjacent trolleys waiting to be pumped out at Strathwells Hospital, lost their driving licences at the same time and generally slid down life's slippery slope together.

'I've never said this to you but I'd dearly love to give up the booze as well. My liver is shot and I hate making such a bloody fool of myself all the time. What else have you found? Is it the padre? Must speak to him.'

'It's no' the padre, Jock, although he does stay in touch. It's this stuff.' Campbell pulled a small polythene envelope from the top pocket of his lumberjack shirt. 'Take a look.'

Jock took the envelope and his eyes squinted as he peered in and sniffed it. 'Smells like an OXO cube; looks like dried nettles. What is it?'

Campbell leaned forward conspiratorially and whispered, 'Cannabis.'

'Cannabis, eh? Where d'you get it from?'

'In a field less than a mile from here. I came across it a week ago when taking a short cut home. I passed oot in the middle of the field and when I woke up I recognized it was the stuff that Dr Mackenzie recommended to get me off the whisky. Geordie Kinloch is growing it but isnae registered, so he won't report anything. Rory Dallas says it's OK to help myself, as long as I don't talk to anyone. But I thought you'd be interested.'

'Geordie Kinloch, eh? What a rogue. He always comes across as squeaky clean. What's he doing growing cannabis?'

'They say he found a bag o' seed on the road up in the glens. Must ha' been dropped by old Fleming. He has a deal with a pharma company to grow it for their medicines. He's the only registered grower in the county.'

'Well I'll be damned. Can you take me to the field? I'll pick up a couple of black bin bags at the castle on the way over. And I'll join you in a ginger beer.'

The best route to Hatton Field was to strike out across country due north of Mormaer Castle. There was a woodland walk through stands of Douglas fir, leading across a stone bridge, into a birch plantation and across one of Geordie Kinloch's fields, adjacent to Hatton Field. As the crow flew it was less than a mile and the old boozing pals bantered happily all the way.

'Good Lord, Campbell,' Jock exclaimed when he beheld the field of vigorous cannabis plants nodding happily in the summer breeze, 'this'll make up for any shortfall in the Single Farm Payment.'

'Aye, it will that. Here, let me help ye fill those bags. It needs to be dried for a few days, then it crumbles and you can smoke it, chew it or crumble and cook with it. I tell ye, my liver's ne'er felt so good, Jock.'

'Well, I'll try anything to get off the booze. The countess'll be thrilled, if I can persuade her to come back and live with me.'

They filled the two black plastic bags with cannabis leaves, slung them over their shoulders like two burglars from a cartoon strip and tramped back to Mormaer Castle. They dumped the bags in the entrance hall by a selection of cricket bats, stuffed birds and stags' heads, croquet mallets, curling stones and snow shoes.

'I'll get the key to the game larder. We don't use it for hanging game any more – bloody Health and Safety wallahs – so it'll be a perfect spot to hang this stuff to dry.'

Jock returned with an eighteenth-century iron key. 'Follow me.'

They carried the bags to a slatted stone outhouse three hundred yards downwind of the castle by a towering beech tree. Jock opened the door with a lot of clunking and scraping. Sweeping spiders' webs from their faces they entered a cold, breezy, empty chamber with dozens of iron hooks hanging from the ceiling.

'Absolutely perfect. Campbell, can you get going and hang this stuff on the hooks for me? When you're done, come in and have a wh…er – a cup of tea.'

'Of course I'll do it for ye, but I need to get away afterwards. It'll take a couple of weeks to dry. Mine only took a few days because I hung it above my stove.'

'Fair enough. Will you come back and taste it with me in a couple of weeks?'

'Aye Jock. I'll see you then.'

The word about Kinloch's miraculous field passed around the villages and surrounding communities of Invermore and Mormaer like wildfire. It was odd, considering that PC Dallas, Johnnie, Campbell, Kinloch and Jock the Earl were the only ones who really knew. They had no interest in publicizing their discovery, any more than the man who triggered the 1849 Gold Rush in California had in telling the world about finding gold in the Sierras.

There was a remarkable increase in local folks exercising their Right to Roam across Kinloch's land. When challenged by Johnnie as they walked across growing crops towards Hatton Field, they triumphantly told him, 'Fokk away off, Johnnie. There's nae sich thing as private anymore. The Law says so.' Johnnie patiently replied that the Outdoor Access Code said no such thing. But there was no telling them, so he resorted to a more traditional method of persuasion, the cocked shotgun. At least this kept the folks to the footpaths.

After such a day of sightseers and samplers wandering around the farm, PC Dallas called Kinloch. 'Your immunity is stretching very thin, Geordie. Might I suggest that you flail the crop, burn it and plough it back into the field as a matter of urgency?'

'It's being flailed this afternoon, Rory. We'll rake it up and burn it as soon as it's dry. If this weather continues it should be ready to burn by Saturday.'

'Good. Don't delay any longer. I want this whole thing to be over as quickly as possible before it gets out of control.'

'It's as good as done.'

The residue of flailed cannabis plants was raked into a high pile like a traditional haystack, guarded around the clock by Johnnie. He pitched a small tent beside his 'dopestack', as he proudly described it, and fended off all comers. The material was still damp and would need several days before it would be dry enough to ignite.

The village grapevine not only knew the day, but the hour, at which Johnnie's dopestack would be set on fire. Groups of villagers gathered at the edge of Hatton Field, downwind of the stack, singly at first, then in twos and threes, then in groups of half a dozen. By seven o'clock that Saturday evening there were scores of people hanging around in excited anticipation of the bonfire.

Kinloch arrived in the Land Rover, felt the pile of vegetation for humidity and nodded to Johnnie, who had earlier stuffed a pile of old newspapers into the heart of the stack and left a fuse of twisted paper to light them by.

Kinloch struck a match and lit the fuse. A wisp of smoke curled into the evening air, followed by crackling as the dry vegetation caught fire. By the time fire reached the newspapers a thick plume was billowing into the sky and blowing towards the onlookers. Instead of dodging the smoke, they turned their faces into it, much as a sunflower turns its face to follow the sun. They converged into a tight group where the smoke was thickest, holding hands and singing as they inhaled the smoke. One of the villagers had brought a Boom Box and the scene was accompanied by Original Hits of the Sixties. Some giggled and others rolled on the ground, helpless with laughter. Some threw off their clothes and danced in the warm air, convulsed with mirth. Johnnie and Kinloch carefully kept upwind of the smoke, and with the eye of a sober caretaker supervising a drunken party, Kinloch began to worry.

'The fire's going to be like this for at least another hour and these people will be asphyxiated by then. We can't just let them keep inhaling the fumes. We've created the world's biggest joint and there are about seventy very high villagers rolling around in the grass.'

'Aye, this is Invermore's Woodstock right enough,' Johnnie was grinning and began to giggle.

'Don't you go too, Johnnie. Keep out of the smoke whatever you do.'

'Aye, keep oot the smoke. How aboot this?' He stuck his face straight into the thickest column of fumes and came out with a grin that Kinloch did not imagine he possessed.

'Johnnie, don't be such an idiot.'

At that moment, two figures emerged behind Kinloch. 'Hey, you didn't tell us you were having a party.' It was the voice of Jock the Earl. He was accompanied by Campbell who repeated, 'Aye, you didn't tell us you were having a party.' Before Kinloch could say anything, the two of them started to run towards the pile of giggling humanity in the smoke and cast off their clothes like kids arriving at the beach.

Johnnie, who had stood grinning behind Kinloch, shouted, 'Hey, what the fokk, I'm joining in too. Come on Geordie, dinnae be such an old woman.'

Kinloch felt light headed and was beginning to float above the field into one of the surrounding trees. He looked down at the scene and began to giggle uncontrollably. The fire was past its peak but everyone was dancing to the sound of the Beatles on the soft grass.

He sang to the tune of *Lucy in the Sky with Diamonds*, 'It's a hell of a party... Invermore's never seen anything like it... How on earth did they know...? Got to plough the field again tomorrow... This'll never happen again here... *Carpe diem...* that's it...! *Carpe diem...*'

Geordie was on the brink of discarding his jacket and entering the fray when he saw the police Land Rover bumping across the field towards him. It stopped and PC Dallas stepped out, dressed in his full constable's regalia. Josie was sitting in the passenger seat, looking amused.

'Good evening Geordie. A pall of smoke was reported in this area. I'm just checking that everything is all right.'

'Everything is just fine. Tomorrow we plough this field. Experiment over.'

'Glad to hear it. Enjoy your evening, sir.' PC Dallas had a smile in his eyes and winked.

'I think it's a bit late for that now,' Geordie replied. Josie put her arm around his and they headed unsteadily back home across the fields.

Layout: Stephen M.L. Young
                 latouveilhe@mac.com

Font: Adobe Garamond (11pt)

Copies of this book can be ordered via the Internet:

                 www.librario.com

or from:

                 Librario Publishing Ltd
                 Brough House
                 Milton Brodie
                 Kinloss
                 Moray IV36 2UA
                 Tel /Fax No 01343 850 617